I0640264

Florida Heat
David Huff

Publisher: David Huff Publishing—Ephraim, UT
ISBN: 978-0-9988003-1-8
Card Catalogue Number: 2017913056
Florida Heat/ David Huff
Digital distribution | David Huff, 2017.
Paperback | David Huff | 2017

DEDICATION

For Reed and Crystal, Mariah and CJ, Rachael and Lucas, and our grandkids, and the joy we receive from having them in our lives. And last of all, my greatest fan in life and in the eternities to come, Linda who is my hero and confidant and the one I get to spend my life with forever. If I get into heaven it will be because of you.

Found in a crushed fortune cookie:

You don't become a failure until you're satisfied with being one.

CHAPTER I

The man was running through the jungles of Colombia trying to stay ahead of the men pursuing him. The trail ahead of him was the only clearing through the jungle, and he knew that trail would lead to a small village and onto the river.

"If I can make it to the river and grab a canoe, I'll be able to escape from the men following me," he thought to himself.

As he was making his way on the trail, he heard the report of a rifle and he hit the ground, rolling into the jungle. A bullet whizzed over his shoulder into the dense foliage in front of him. He thought they must be getting closer, too close for comfort. The man dived into the jungle on his left and made a trail through the brush. It would be slow going for him but also slow going for the pursuers. When he found a small clearing, he stopped and listened, hoping he wouldn't hear the men chasing him. As he sat collecting his thoughts and catching his breath, he stayed in the shadows of the green jungle to conceal himself from the prying eyes that were looking for him. The man pulled out his sat phone and made a call to his handler; after the second ring the handler answered the phone.

"Oscar 1 reporting in, situation Tabasco, repeat Tabasco, need extract immediately," the man said.

"Affirmative situation Tabasco, pick you up at designated spot 24 hours," the man on the other end of the sat phone said.

With that, the man put his phone away and listened again, more intently this time-- no noise, no sounds. As he stood up, he got his directions and made his way deeper into the jungle. He had 24 hours to get to the extraction point, which by all accounts was a good 10 miles east from where he thought he was. In the jungle, unless you were to climb a tree, it was easy to get lost. In fact, the jungle can be so thick you can't see the sun at midday. The man had a compass to help him in his journey to make it to the extraction point. He figured if he kept going east he would run into the river, and from there it would be easy to make it to the extraction point. He then heard the voices of the men following him. He looked around for an opening in the jungle to start making his way through. At first it looked like shadows playing on the broad leaves, but as he looked a little more closely, he saw what he was looking for. Quickly making his way to the shadows, he saw the opening into the jungle and he went into it. Having been raised in the South American jungles in Uruguay, he knew his way and was careful not to do anything that would give away his position.

Having gone to America to go to college, he had been recruited by the Drug Enforcement Agency (DEA) to go back to the jungles in his homeland and help eradicate the drug problems in his country; specifically, to find the labs used to develop heroin and cocaine. At first when approached, he was leery about getting involved. Only after receiving a letter from his sister telling how his best friend, who had been farming poppy plants to make money to live on, had died when a rival gang came in and killed him for the drugs he had on hand, he changed his mind and said yes. After being accepted into the DEA the man went to the DEA academy at Quantico, Virginia, that was 18 weeks long. The training included physical fitness training, hand-to-hand combat, shooting techniques and the academics of legal search and seizure, proper arrest techniques, business ethics and basic law. The man then attended the international training for working with other international drug enforcement organizations to learn how they operate and to assist in their operations.

By the time the training was done the man was sent to Colombia, South America, to start his career. He had been assigned to Colombia for approximately two years, and the excitement of being a new agent ready to take on the world became a routine of looking for the poppy farms and listening to the people in the villages for any clues that would indicate new poppy farms being created or when the couriers were picking up the morphine bricks to deliver to the cartels.

This is why the man was being chased through the jungle and was hiding out. His point of contact had seen a new poppy farm from the helicopter photos and asked the man to check it out. The task was to go in and take pictures of the setup and return without being seen. The helicopter dropped him off about two miles from where the morphine farm was supposed to be, and from there he walked into the jungle looking for the farm. If everything went well, he would get the pictures. He would then phone his contact and they would come and get him. They in turn would send the photos to the next level of command. At that point the next step would be to determine the next course of action, which would be to either destroy the farm or wait and see which cartel was running it. But on his way out he tripped aground sensor, which alerted the security team. Now things had changed and he was on the run, so the pictures were now a moot point. The man's only thought was to get back to someplace safe. As he made his way through the jungle, he would stop and listen to hear if anybody was close by. After about an hour of tough going he figured he had escaped them or they had quit chasing him. It was about three in the afternoon when he stopped and checked his compass. He was still headed east towards the river. Eventually, he would get to the river and make his way down river to a bigger city. At this time, he knew his chances of getting to the extraction point in time to be picked up were slim, and he knew his best chance of survival was to try to walk out of the jungle. With no food or water, he figured it would be a long shot making it out alive. The man knew he could survive in the jungle if he kept his head and just kept moving forward. The question now was, how long would it take to get home safe?

Sleeping on the ground created its own kind of problems, as would sleeping in the trees; however, the trees were safer than the ground at night, unless he could find a cave and build a fire at the entrance to keep the animals at bay. In the supplies he brought with him were matches, a hunting knife with a six-inch blade and, of course, a compass. His clothes and boots were sturdy and strong to handle the heat and moisture of the jungle. For all intents and purposes, he could survive if he kept his head and kept moving forward.

As he made his way towards the river, not knowing how far it was, it started to rain; and with the rain came fresh water and the flash floods that would turn a small creek or river into a storming flood. Knowing this, he stayed to the high ground watching the ridges around him, just in case they were still looking for him. With the rain the trail was slippery and he had to hang onto the foliage in order not to lose his footing and go down the side of the mountain, possibly breaking a leg or killing himself from the fall. This made the going a little slower than he had planned, but there was nothing that he could do about it. As he continued through the rain, he came upon a cave and used it to get himself dry and stay for the night. As the man sat there looking out of the cave and watching the rain, he thought to himself how nice it would be to be back at his bungalow, dry and warm, drinking a tall glass of beer. He knew the storm would be over in about another hour; it rained like this every day during the wet season. This was something he had grown up with as a child in his homeland of Uruguay.

In its own way, there was a comfort being out here in the wild jungle with rain falling all around that brought a peacefulness to his mind; in a sense, he was at home in the jungle.

Chapter II

The sun was just starting to come up over the Chiricahua Mountains; the first light of the morning was starting to filter through the curtains of the bedroom. Buck was the first to move, trying not to disturb Rachael as she slept next to him. They had been married a year and they still felt as if it was the first week of marriage. Buck had decided he liked being married and liked the idea of having someone to take care of. The weight of being married started to show around his belly; all his shirts were beginning to shrink around his midriff area. He knew that as the Sheriff of Smith County, this would not do for his people to see him like this. Fit and trim, lean and mean, hard as nails, ready for a fight was the image he needed to have to inspire and lead his deputies. However, exercise would have to wait until at least tomorrow or until he had his first coffee. He walked into the kitchen, started the coffee maker, and headed into the bathroom to take a shower, figuring when he was done with the shower the coffee would be ready.

7

As he sat drinking his coffee, Rachael walked into the kitchen and came and sat down on his lap.

Nuzzling his ear, she asked, "What are doing up so early this morning?"

"I have a meeting with the city council at 9:00 this morning. "

She started blowing on his neck; this drove Buck nuts. "You sure you need to be at the meeting at 9:00?"

With that, Buck picked her up and, as she was giggling, he tossed her on the bed and said, "Oh, for the good days when I was a just a deputy."

"O.K., Mr. Sheriff, I understand; duty calls and I'll be waiting for you when you get home." She laughed.

Buck looked at her and smiled. "Just like that, don't you move until I get back, you promise?"

"I promise," Rachael yelled as Buck walked towards the front door.

When the meeting with the city council was over, Buck drove to his office and checked in with his secretary to see if anything exciting was going on that needed his attention. The secretary jumped up from her desk and had a number of phone messages in her hand. Buck made his way towards his desk with the secretary following him, talking to him the whole time about the phone calls. Buck sat down and listened to her as she read off the list of calls. Most of the calls dealt with incidents from the night before, and he would let his senior deputies handle them. He was looking at the incident report from the night before when the secretary read a phone message from the FBI with a "Call me when you get a chance."

"Stop," Buck said to the secretary, "please read that to me again."

"FBI message: Please contact me as soon as possible."

"Is there a name on it?"

"The voice said you would know who it was."

Buck sat there thinking about the message from the FBI. The secretary continued with the phone messages that she had received for him. All Buck could think was he hadn't worked with the FBI for over a year since Rachael had been an FBI agent and they had worked on the bank robbery and double murders together. That was when he met Rachael for the first time. At this point the secretary had left and came back again with a cup of coffee in her hand.

Buck looked up at her and said, "Thank you; let me look at that message from the FBI."

The secretary dutifully brought the message with her, along with the coffee. When Buck looked at the phone number, the area code was from Florida. He thought it couldn't be from FBI man Evans, could it? His memories of that time seemed to flood back to him as if it were yesterday. A lot had happened since then-- becoming sheriff after a recall vote was done, the old sheriff being sent to a maximum-security prison near Phoenix. Buck remembered the press had a field day with the Smith County Sheriff's Department over all of that. Buck had married Rachael and she had quit the FBI to work with the new sheriff/husband as a new captain in the sheriff's office. Since then, they had moved and bought a house to be closer to the county seat. All in all, everything worked out good for his and her careers. He sat there thinking about all of this when the phone on his desk rang.

He picked it up. "Hello."

"You want to meet for lunch?" Rachael asked.

"That would be fine; let's say around 1:00?"

Rachael agreed. "I have some errands to run before that and I'll meet you at our favorite place."

With that, he hung up the phone and sat there, still deep in thought about the message. He would tell Rachael about the message from the FBI over lunch.

The day-to-day job started to work in his mind, thus requiring his attention. By 1:00 he was ready to get away from it all. He had often thought he had done a favor to the old sheriff by locking him up and getting him away from the phones and meetings that now he had to deal with. Buck chuckled to himself, thinking better here in this prison without walls than there in the prison with walls and assorted other bad guys.

He was to meet Rachael at their favorite café in town and, as usual, he was running late and she was on time.

As she sat patiently waiting, the waitress asked her, "Do you want the usual?"

Rachael recognized the waitress and said, "Why, how did you know that?" and laughed.

"Just a wild guess," the waitress said as she laughed.

Buck walked in on the laughing ladies and surmised they were laughing at him for being late once more. He smiled and sat down next to Rachael.

After the waitress left, he looked at Rachael and said, "I'm sorry for being late again, as usual."

"Not to worry; the waitress has our order, the usual."

"Are we that predictable here?"

She smiled at him. "So how is your day so far?"

"Same old stuff, different day, with the exception of a call from Evans at the FBI."

Rachael looked surprised at hearing about the phone call and asked, "What does he want?"

"I don't know; I've not returned his call yet. I think he might want to talk to both of us."

They chitchatted over lunch, but the elephant in the room was the phone call from Evans.

After lunch Rachael asked, "Are you going to call him this afternoon?"

"Yes, would you like to be there for the call?"

She thought a moment and said, "Yes, I would, as a matter of fact, like to be there. I'll follow you back to work."

When lunch was done, she followed him to the office. Once again, the secretary had a few messages for him, and as he looked them over he sat down and left them on his desk. He looked on his desk for the message from Evans and finally found it. He dialed the number and put it on speaker phone so Rachael could hear the conversation as well.

After the third ring Evans answered the phone, "Special Agent Evans in charge, Miami office."

Rachael and Buck both said, "Hello, how's it going down in Miami? Do you have a suntan yet?"

Upon recognizing the two voices on the other end, he laughed. "I'm almost too important to get a suntan; besides, I'm so busy I haven't had time to be like you guys sitting around with nothing to do."

They all laughed at this.

"I'm gaining weight and it isn't from Rachael's cooking, either," Buck replied.

Evans laughed even harder at what Buck had said. "Do you at least get the couch at night for that remark?"

"No, he doesn't; he goes straight to the doghouse," Rachael replied.

"So you guys have a dog now?" Evans asked.

"No, not yet," Buck replied.

They all laughed again at that.

"So what's our favorite FBI agent calling us for?" asked Buck.

With that question Evans got serious. "Can both of you come down to Miami sometime in the next couple of days?"

Buck looked at Rachael. "Let me look into my schedule for the week, and we'll let you know for sure."

"That would be great, and please don't tell anyone about it; I'll explain it better when you both get here," Evans said.

After Buck hung up the phone he looked at Rachael. "Pretty spooky, don't you think?"

"I don't know what to think. What are we going to tell everybody here about our sudden trip to Miami?"

Buck walked around his desk and hugged her, saying, "You know, we haven't had our honeymoon yet and Miami sounds like a great place to have one. Everything here is pretty slow right now--no investigations going on and no court dates coming up."

Buck called the secretary in and checked with her about the schedule for the following two weeks, and as she looked over the schedule book, nothing stood out. With that, Buck and Rachael made plans to go to Miami for a honeymoon.

CHAPTER III

On the day of their flight Rachael and Buck got to the airport two hours early. After their baggage was checked in and they had gone through security, they sat watching the TV near their gate while waiting to board the plane. Both were sipping some coffee and eating a breakfast sandwich. The drive to the airport started early in the morning around 4:00 am. Both were excited to go to Miami; this would be their first trip together since being married. Buck looked around the concourse and noticed everybody walking through was in a hurry to get to their gates to sit and wait.

Buck looked around at the people who would be flying with them and said, "Ahhh, the jet set, road warriors, people in a hurry to go where they need to go in order to relax."

"The good life, being in motion and going nowhere."

Neither one of them missed this life of being on the go and never being able to settle down, more so Rachael than Buck.

When they got on the airplane, they both found the seats uncomfortable and too close to the seat in front of them.

"At least, we didn't have to pay for the flight to Miami," Buck said as he looked at Rachael.

"Oh yeah, remind me again," Rachael said as she was trying to get comfortable in her seat.

The flight to Miami was uneventful and was only three hours long. When they stepped out of the tunnel, Evans was waiting for them and took them to the carousel to get their luggage. Once inside Evans car, Buck noticed the AC was on full blast.

Evans looked at him and said, smiling, "Yes, it's hot but it's a wet hot."

Buck and Rachael laughed at the remark. It was a short distance to the federal building in Miami and before long they were in Evans' office.

"Wow," was all that Rachael could say about the office.

It was spacious with a desk at one end and a table and chairs halfway to the other end with a couch, love seat and a big screen TV at the other end of the room.

"Our tax dollars at work," Buck said as he was looking around.

"I heard that. Ahhh, the good life comes to the federal employee," Evans said as he came through the door.

Evans motioned Buck and Rachael to the couch area of the room and gestured for them to sit down.

As they made themselves comfortable on the couch, Buck asked, "What was so terribly important that you needed us to be here in Miami; why all the hush-hush stuff?"

"First of all, I apologize for the secrecy, I thought it expedient to keep it on the down low, at least until we met," Evans said. He then proceeded to tell them, "The reason I called you guys is because we need your help in finding a poppy field in Honduras. We have heard talk about a field growing there for quite some time now. We just don't know where it is. That's where you come in. I liked the idea of you being on a honeymoon and that will work for you in Honduras."

Buck and Rachael looked at Evans, surprised by what he was asking.

"You want us to go to Honduras and find a poppy field? You don't have any agents that can do that from here?" Buck asked.

Evans looked at them both, "We have a leak that's feeding our Intel to the cartel in Colombia, who we think is overseeing the Honduras operation. We have sent our own people down there, but they were found out and either sent back or found dead."

Rachael looked at Buck. "But you promised me days lounging on the beach working on my tan, eating at the restaurants and dancing till morning."

Buck and Evans smiled at her.

"We don't know where the leak is; hence, that is why we kept you guys on the down low. We couldn't afford to lose you guys through regular channels. Besides, I know I can trust you to do what's right and nobody knows you're here, except Linda," Evans continued.

Evans went to his desk and, using the intercom, he asked the secretary to send Linda into his office. When Linda opened the door and saw who was sitting on the couch, she smiled, reached out, and shook Buck's hand and hugged Rachael.

Looking them over, she said, "Man, you guys are a sight for sore eyes. How have you been doing?"

"We've been doing fine; how about you?" Rachael replied.

"Well, I don't really know. I work for this guy who is a slave driver and never lets me take any days off. In fact, it has gotten so bad working for him that he can't live without me, so out of pity I decided to save him by marrying him and I'm not sure that will be enough," Linda said as she looked at Evans.

Hearing the news, Buck and Rachael looked surprised and were happy for both of them.

"She's right, I can't live without her; I can't even get my stuff together without her," Evans said.

"When is the date?" Rachael asked.

"We were hoping for an October wedding. Will you guys please come?" Linda asked.

Buck looked at Rachael, "We wouldn't miss it for the world."

"Isn't she beautiful?" Evans said as he looked at Linda.

"So was Buck until I married him. Look at him now; he's getting fat," Rachael said.

"Watch out, Evans; the same thing will happen to you," Buck warned.

"It already has." Evans laughed.

With all the catching up done, Evans went back to his brief on Honduras and asked Linda to fill in the blanks for him.

Linda started off by saying, "We have our DEA resources in Colombia and their man was checking into a new poppy farm when he was found out. He called for an extraction, but he never showed up at the appointed time. We think our leak knew about him and set him up to get killed. All of this is pure conjecture right now; we don't know anything for sure. For all we know, he is still alive in the jungle and that's the problem; we need to know where he is and, if he is still alive, get him out."

Buck looked puzzled. "So how does this tie into Honduras and us going there?"

"We think the cartel that is operating in Honduras is the same one that the DEA agent was checking on in Colombia. If we can tie these two operations together, we may be able to find our man and bring him home. There are enough resources from the countries' governments to help us. If it's a new operation with no ties to the cartel, then we would know we have a new player in the arena. Right now, if we send any more of our people in either place, we risk losing our assets on the ground. You guys are unknown to the Intel community and being on a honeymoon will give you the cover you need without raising any kind of suspicion," Linda replied.

"So what do you think?" Evans asked.

"Are we alone out there? And who do we report to if and when we find the poppy farm?" Buck asked.

"For all practical purposes you will be alone, and if you find the farm, you report back to me as quick as you can. We'll do the rest from here," Evans said.

It was Rachael's turn to ask the next question. "How long do we have to find it?"

"The island is small and it shouldn't take you more than a week or two to locate it. Look at it this way: It's a two- week paid vacation in the heart of the jungle," Linda said.

"Well, why didn't you say so? We're ready to spend your money anytime. What will we need to keep in touch with you and when do we leave?" Buck asked.

Evans and Linda looked at both of them and said thanks to Buck and Rachael.

"We have a hotel room for you tonight and we'll get your stuff ready for tomorrow morning. We should have you ready to go by tomorrow afternoon. We'll get your plane tickets set up for the last flight going out tomorrow night. For tonight we're going to treat you both to dinner at our place and I guarantee the cook is excellent there," Evans said.

With everything taken care of, Evans asked the secretary to handle all of the lodging details for Buck and Rachael.

"We took the liberty of taking your bags to the hotel already, so they should be in your room when you get there. We'll pick you up around 6:30 pm for dinner, which should give you a chance to enjoy Miami for a couple of hours and get a suntan by the pool," Linda said.

"It don't get any better than this." Rachael smiled.

"No siree only the best from our government." Buck added.

"Get out of here before I change my mind," Evans said.

As Buck and Rachael walked out, the secretary intercepted them. "A car is downstairs waiting to take you to the hotel where you will be staying, and the same car will pick you up in the morning around 8:00."

With that they went downstairs to the front of the federal building. The driver with the car showed up and took them to the hotel. The ride lasted about 15 minutes, and Buck and Rachael didn't say a word the whole-time riding in the back of the car. The driver dropped them off at the front of the hotel and left without a word. They walked up to the front desk to get the keys to their room. After identifying themselves, the person at the front desk gave them their keys and showed them to their room.

Once they were in the room, Buck looked at Rachael and asked, "Are we crazy for doing this?"

"Look at it this way; we get an all-expenses-paid trip to go on a honeymoon to look at the sights of the island and then go home. What could go wrong with something like that?"

"That's what has me worried about this sightseeing tour."

Buck and Rachael freshened up and headed out to see the sights and sounds of Miami and the beaches nearby. They stopped at an outdoor café, ordered some iced tea, and sat under the umbrella looking at all the people passing by.

"I could get used to this kind of life here on the beach," Buck said as he was watching the girls in their bikinis.

"It's really going to be hard getting used to this life when you can't walk anymore."

"Yes, Ma'am, three bagsful Sir, Ma'am." Buck said as he feigned being scared at her remark.

Rachael laughed at him as he saluted her. Later that evening Evans and Linda picked them up for dinner and took them back to their place. As Evans grilled the steaks, Buck was talking to him about the life here in Miami. While they talked Rachael and Linda were talking about the engagement ring that Evans had given her and about the upcoming October wedding.

While Buck was outside with Evans he asked, "How bad can this get in Honduras?"

Evans stood there thinking about the question for a moment before answering. "If everything goes right, it should be easy in, easy out. If it goes bad, it's hard to say. You'll be on your own, with the exception of us monitoring the communications link. But aside from me and Linda, nobody knows why you're really there. All I can say is trust no one while you're there and just be careful. If necessary, we can come and get you; but if we do, it may blow our presence there."

Buck thought for a moment about what Evans had said, offering to turn the steaks on the grill for him while Evans went in to get the plates to put the meat on. After dinner they went and saw some of the nightlife in Miami. About 11:00 pm, Evans and Linda drove them to their hotel and dropped them off in front. When the car had driven off, Rachael reached over and kissed Buck and snuggled into his arm. They walked that way all the way back to their room. As Buck opened the door to the room he quickly picked up Rachael and carried her over the threshold and said, laughing, "Our first night together." With that, he closed the door.

CHAPTER IV

The next morning after breakfast Buck and Rachael were outside and waiting when the car came and picked them up to take them to the federal building. Buck and Rachael sat in the back of the Crown Victoria and looked out the windows as the driver bypassed all of the traffic tie-ups. Within minutes the car was at the front of the federal building. After getting out they stood there for a moment and looked at each other.

"And so it begins," Buck said.

Rachael nodded as she turned to go up the steps to the front door with Buck following behind her. When they reached the metal detectors, Evans was waiting for them on the other side.

"I see you two survived last night," He said.

"We're really not sure we did; for a while there it was touch and go," Buck said.

Evans laughed, as did Buck and Rachael.

"It was rough. These people showed up and took us to dinner, and I don't remember anything after that; it's all a blur from there," Rachael said, smiling.

"You can't be too careful in the big city nowadays," Evans laughed.

With that, they walked to the elevator and rode it up to the second floor.

"This is our Q area," said Evans, referring to a spy and all of the gadgets he used from Q. With a special card passed through the slide, the steel-frame door opened to let them in. Inside was what looked like a laboratory used in the old Frankenstein movies. Further down was a display of different kinds of equipment hanging on the wall. You could hear gunfire coming from another closed door.

"Our indoor firing range is beyond that door and where we test different weapons," Evans said.

As they continued walking down the hallway, they came to a room where there was a guard stationed in front. The door had a retina scan you used to get in. After scanning Evans' eyes, the door slid open and they all walked through. Inside the room the lights were low so as to not disturb the people working there. There was a computer about the size of an old cigarette machine standing in the corner of the room. There were two people seated at consoles monitoring the screens in front of them. They were watching an airplane flying across the Caribbean Ocean; it was a small Cessna flying towards the coastline of Honduras. Against the wall was a big screen with the outline of the southern part of the U.S. showing southern Texas, all of western Florida, the East and West Indies all the way across to Mexico and Guatemala down to the top of South America. Both Buck and Rachael were amazed at what they saw.

Evans started to speak. "This is our nerve center for all of the air traffic that flies into and out of anywhere from the southern part of the United States. If you look closely on the other wall, you will see another screen like this, except it tracks the comings and goings of the shipping lanes. With geosynchronous satellite coverage we can identify all of the air and sea traffic in this area within seconds to determine if they are friendlies or the bad guys carrying drugs. We work closely with Homestead Air Force Base and the U.S. Coast Guard when identifying unknowns in the area both on the sea and airborne. As you can tell, nothing happens in the area without us knowing about it." Both Buck and Rachael were thinking WOW, who would have known.

"We will be watching you via satellite and tracking you by GPS the whole time you're moving around exploring Honduras," Evans said.

Handing them cell phones to carry, Evans told them, "These new cell phones are set up so that we can follow you via satellite, with a special GPS signal that only our spy in the sky can follow. The drug cartel's equipment for tracking is almost as sophisticated as ours. The only difference is that with ours we can tell when they go to the bathroom and who went."

Both Buck and Rachael laughed at the comment Evans had made. Still standing in awe, Evans let it all sink in for the two.

"Are you ready to go?" Evans asked.

With that, they left the nerve center and walked out the same door they had come in. Once their eyes got accustomed to the light again, they noticed a man standing there with a folder in his hand. Evans grabbed the folder and opened it up and then handed them the contents.

"Here are your round-trip plane tickets, your hotel accommodations and a rental car for your use. As we agreed to before, you are newlyweds on your honeymoon. For things to do in the area there is scuba diving, snorkeling, zip lines, bus tours, fishing, canoeing, kayaking and, of course, exploring the jungles. You'll be flying into Ramón Villeda Morales International Airport and from there you will get your car rental and drive to your hotel. The lodge and spa at East and West Park are on the northern tip of Honduras towards the ocean; it's quite a beautiful area of Honduras. I almost wish I was going there with Linda myself."

"It's not too late to join us," Buck offered.

"Maybe next time. Enclosed you will find a map of the country showing all of the places that could be used for growing the poppies. As you already know, the location of the poppies will have to be out of sight from the general population so as not to create problems for the growers. I suggest you look in the less populated areas of Honduras, possibly in the mountainous areas of the country," Evans said.

As Buck and Rachael followed Evans, they were met by Linda at the door leading into the room.

"I just wanted to say goodbye and good luck on your honeymoon trip," She said, hugging both of them.

"One final thing, we, of course, cannot give you any weapons to take with you; however, that being said, you will find some protection when you arrive at your room. Just look inside the back of the bathroom closet," Evans said.

"Let us know when you get there. Just pretend you're calling your parents to let us know you got there safe and sound; you know how we worry about your kids;" Linda added.

They all laughed at her comment.

"You have any questions?" Evans asked.

Buck looked at Rachael and then back to Evans and Linda. "Not at this time, but if I think of something I'll give you a call."

"Good," said Evans as he continued saying, "Our driver will take you back to your hotel so you can pack and get to the airport on time; from this point on you're pretty much on your own."

With that, Evans shook Buck's hand and hugged Rachael. "We really do appreciate what you're doing for us. Remember we have a leak here; don't trust anyone except myself and Linda. At the slightest hint of trouble, get out of there fast. Linda would never forgive me or herself if you guys got hurt on your honeymoon."

"Neither would we," Rachael replied, laughing.

As Evans walked them to the front of the federal-building foyer, the driver was waiting for them. Evans and Linda said their goodbyes and were gone. The driver led them to the Crown Victoria in the parking lot and left for their hotel. After loading their suitcases into the trunk of the car, the driver took them to the Miami International Airport, where they checked into the Aero México ticket counter.

"Well, what you think about all of this?" Buck asked as they made their way to the gate for their flight.

"It should be fun--sightseeing, scuba diving and snorkeling."

"My thought exactly."

When the person at the gate called for the passengers to start boarding, Rachael looked apprehensive and leaned into Buck and whispered into his ear, "I love you."

"I love you too, and I won't let anything happen to you."

She grabbed his hand and smiled, "I'm not worried about me; I'm worried about you."

The two-and-a-half-hour flight to Honduras was barely enough time to doze on the plane. When they retrieved their luggage and found their car, they swapped it for an SUV, just in case they needed to mountain-climb in their search for the poppy farm. On the way out of the airport they drove through some of the slums of the city. As they drove by, Buck couldn't help but notice how poor the people were.

"No wonder the drug cartel is making inroads into these people's lives. Starvation is a very poor hobby and any kind of money would help, no matter where it came from."

"You can't help but feel sorry for these people."

It took them an hour to find their way to the East and West Lodge, where they were staying. The roads were covered with a green canopy of trees and plants everywhere. When they drove into the area of the lodge, they parked their SUV in front and walked down a wooden-plank sidewalk to the front desk. The jungle foliage was so thick you could get lost in it five minutes from anywhere in the lodge area. The trees were alive with different kinds of birds and monkeys. There was also a beautiful crystal-white beach on the other side of the lodge. The lobby had polished wood flooring with a rock entrance covered with baskets of flowers everywhere. The hummingbirds were flying around the flowers busily drinking the sweet nectar from the plants. The inner walls were made of rock and when they reached the ceiling, there was a one-foot gap between the walls and ceiling. This would allow the cool air during the rain to come through and cool the foyer down to a comfortable temperature.

Rachael looked at the place and saw how beautiful it was. "Pinch me; I think I'm in heaven."

All Buck could do was stare. In all his time in Arizona he had never seen anything like this before in his life.

"May I help you?" The front-desk receptionist asked.

"We have reservations under the name of Mr. and Mrs. Buck Tanner," Buck said.

The reservationist looked and found their reservation and rang the bell for the boy to grab their luggage from the SUV.

"Welcome, we hope you enjoy your stay and if there is anything you need, please feel free to call the front desk and we'll do what we can for you."

"In fact, this is our first time here and I was wondering, do you have a map of the surrounding area outside of these grounds in case we would like to see some of the local sights?" Rachael asked.

The front-desk receptionist gave her a map and a sheet with all of the local areas of interest, bus schedules and sightseeing tours. As the bell boy took them to their cottage, they walked down a manicured rock path to their place.

Upon entering the cottage, they were amazed at the size of their room. Everything was done in a polished wood accent. The bed was a queen size with a bug net to cover the whole bed. The veranda went all the way around the cottage and had a hammock for two on the side where the jungle was. From the veranda, you could hear the howler monkeys playing in the treetops. The room was elegant and the kitchen was the size of an apartment kitchen. The table and chairs were made of wood as well, and all of it matched the walls and bed frame.

"Well, I guess were not in Kansas anymore, Toto," Buck said as he looked around.

"I guess not." Rachael laughed.

After tipping the bell boy and getting their clothes out of the suitcases, they decided to walk around the hotel area. They found the path to the spa, the canoes and kayaks for the river, the pool hall, and the outdoor-and-indoor restaurant. The pool was shaped like a teardrop and the depth at the far end was six feet. The hot tub was big enough for seven or more, depending on the size of the people using it. In all of their years, neither Buck nor Rachael had seen anything so beautiful in their lives. Buck had to keep reminding himself as to why they were here. The quiet of the jungle mixed with the birds and other animal life was enough to take 10 years of stress off of your life. Rachael understood why people loved to come here to get away from it all.

After getting back to their cottage, Buck called Evans and left a message to let him know all was well and that they arrived at the lodge with no problems. Rachael went into the bathroom and rummaged around the cabinet and found two Glock handguns and two extra clips for each one of the handguns. Rachael came out with both guns and handed one of them to Buck with the clips.

"No use going anywhere half naked," She said.

"Besides where would you hide them?" Buck smiled.

The rest of the day they lounged around the hotel grounds eating at the restaurant and enjoying each other's company in their cottage. When nightfall came, a whole new set of sounds came alive from the jungle. You could hear the animals moving about in the tree canopy. As they listened to the night sounds while lying in bed, they were still amazed at how beautiful it was here.

Chapter V

When the sun rose the next morning, Buck and Rachael were already up and dressed for the day. They had been looking at the map trying to determine where to look first for the poppy farm. They knew that for the poppy farm to deliver the best poppies it had to be in the higher elevations and most likely on a mountain. Buck thought of the poppy fields in Afghanistan and the type of terrain they were located in. They decided to look up in the mountains south of the lodge. The giveaway would be the poppy flowers blooming during this time of the year.

Buck and Rachael headed out of their cottage to grab a bite to eat for breakfast. Once they put their order in for breakfast, Buck was reading the map, trying to calculate the miles for going and coming back and how long it would take to do so. Rachael was wondering if they should pack a lunch for their trip. They both started talking at the same time about what they had been thinking about.

They caught themselves doing this twice before Rachael said, "Okay, you first."

Buck, looking at the map said, "I figure we will be going about 100 miles one way to get to this mountain range. Depending on the roads, it could be a short trip or a very long one."

Rachael, thinking about what he was saying, said, "We should probably pack some food for this then."

They both agreed on the extra food and gas, if they could find some.

When the waitress came with their order, Buck asked, "Is there a place to buy gas around here for our SUV?"

The waitress thought a moment and said, "Yes Senor, it's about three kilometers back up the road you came down to get here."

They asked the waitress to prepare two lunches to take with them while they ate their breakfast. After eating they got into their SUV and drove down to the gas station and filled up the SUV and grabbed a few other foodstuffs to take with them. Once squared away for the trip, they headed south into the mountains.

The first hour the driving was easy and comfortable, but the longer they went along the rougher the roads got. In some places, the SUV was looking down into a steep canyon from the passenger side. Rachael held her breath and grabbed the hand grip to keep from falling out. The seatbelts hurt when you took a bounce on some of the potholes and ruts. When they got to a flat place on the road in the canyon, they stopped for lunch. It was a place where you could see for miles in any direction. While Rachael got lunch ready, Buck used his binoculars to look around the canyon walls to find the poppy flowers. After surveying the area for about five minutes and not seeing anything, he put the binoculars away and sat down and ate lunch with Rachael.

"I don't believe the poppy farm is up in this area," Buck said.

"How much more of this road is there?" Rachael asked.

Buck glanced at the map. "Another 10 miles or so. Let's follow the road and when we get to the end, we'll head back to the Ponderosa Little Joe."

"Right partner," Rachael laughed.

They didn't get home until late in the evening, and both of them were tired from being on the road all day. When they got settled and cleaned up, they decided to have dinner in their room. Afterwards, they went to the hot tub just to relax for a while. The water felt good on their muscles and took the aches out of their bodies. Tomorrow would take care of itself; right now it felt good to be back in their cottage again, relaxing in the hot tub. As usual, the birds singing in the morning woke them up. This time they were a little slower getting out of bed. The hot tub last night felt really good and they were able to get a good night's sleep for the first time since flying into Miami. Buck went and got the map of the area and quickly jumped back into bed so they could study the map together staying warm and comfortable. This time they agreed to try east of the lodge to find the poppy farm. After getting dressed, they made their way to the dining room for breakfast.

The same waitress showed up from yesterday to take their order. Rachael asked, "Do you know how to get to this place?" pointing on the map.

The waitress looked at the map. "Yes, I do, but you do not want to go there, a very bad place. Not safe there for you."

"Why not?" Rachael asked, pressing the issue.

"Bad people there, very bad people with guns live there," the waitress said.

"What kind of people?" Rachael asked.

The waitress looked nervous and cast her eyes around the room to make sure nobody was listening to her. "Bad people with guns kill people, especially rich Americans."

Buck put his hand on Rachael's hand as a signal to stop pushing, "Thanks for telling us; we will not go there."

With that, the waitress was back to herself and smiling, asking what they wanted for breakfast. After breakfast, they drove down to the gas station to fill up again and pick up some food for a lunch to eat.

Buck looked at Rachael, "Are you ready for this?"

"Yes," she said as looked at her Glock and chambered around into the gun.

As they made their way up the mountain following the road, they kept a sharp lookout for anything that didn't look right. The road they were on wasn't as bad as the previous day, only shorter. As they followed the road, it ended up being more of a trail than a road. They went as far as they could go in the SUV, then stopped and parked it under some shade trees to hide it from wandering eyes. With the trail, more like an ATV trail, they pressed on, on foot. Carrying their food and water, they kept moving up into the mountain. At one point in their ascent they stopped, and Buck, using his binoculars, scanned the area over. Seeing nothing, once more they kept moving up the mountain. Buck was in the lead when he stopped and dropped to his knees; Rachael did likewise, wondering what was going on. Buck looked at her and using his hands indicated that there were two guys up the road. She looked at him, understanding, and nodded her head and, setting the lunches down, pulled her Glock out. Buck had his out as well. Carefully, half crawling half walking, they moved silently up the trail. Rachael stayed in the shadows of the jungle while Buck continued moving on the trail. When they reached the bend, getting on their stomachs, they started crawling the rest of the way. Looking around the bend in the trail, they both saw from the brush two guys with AK-47s standing there smoking their cigarettes. Buck and Rachael stayed still, watching, and listening to the two men talk. Buck, knowing Spanish, listened to them, even though it was a different dialect from some of the words he knew. From what he could gather, they were talking about their boss and what he wanted to do with the captives they had and talking about what they were going to do with their share of the ransom money.

"They have hostages and are asking for a ransom and talking about what they're going to do with their share," Buck told Rachael.

"We can't let that happen; we need to help if we can."

"We'll follow them, maybe they will lead us to their camp."

After about half an hour, two other guys showed up to relieve them of guard duty. Buck looked at Rachael, using his fingers saying let's follow the two. Rachael agreed and they both slid into the jungle to follow the two men. The big problem they had was getting around the two guards. Waiting a minute, they realized the guards were drunk from drinking some hard, clear liquor from the bottles they had with them. They were more interested in sitting down and trying not to pass out from being drunk. When they finally succumbed to the liquor, Buck and Rachael came up to them and tied their hands behind their backs, took their guns and kept the AKs for their own use. After making sure the guards were incapacitated, they moved up the trail following the other two men.

Walking about a 100 yards, Buck and Rachael could now see the main camp. There must have been 10 guys sitting around a fire with some small buildings on the outside of the camp. Buck watched the camp as Rachael moved to another position directly opposite of him. She waved at Buck to let him know she was in position. They waited patiently for the group of men to settle down and get comfortable. About two hours later, being drunk and tired, the men fell asleep.

Buck was the first to move. With Rachael covering him he went from building to building looking inside to see if there was anybody in the buildings. In the last building Buck checked he found a couple of men sleeping. He motioned to Rachael, letting her know he had found somebody. He studied the two men for a minute to make sure they were being held against their wishes. He could see that they had been beat up and bruised pretty badly.

Buck worked his way around to the door, seeing that there was a piece of wood jammed into the clasp as a lock. He carefully removed the wood and walked into the building where the men were. Moving quickly, he put his hands on their mouths to keep them from making any noise. Once he got their attention, he used his hands to tell them he was helping them escape. The two men seemed relieved about this and were ready to go. Buck motioned for them to stay put while he checked outside the building. Seeing that it was all clear, he nodded to them that it was time to go. They got up, moving as best as they could towards the door, and waited. Buck checked again and led them out of the building, down the trail away from the camp. Rachael followed closely behind, making sure no one followed. When they got to where the guards were, who were still passed out, they beat a path back to the SUV and drove down the mountain. The two men were talking so fast in Spanish that Buck couldn't understand what they were saying. Finally, Buck stopped the SUV and looked at them and using his hands had them slow down so he could understand them. Finally, when they realized what he wanted, they started talking a little slower. Buck learned that they had been kidnapped about a week ago from their businesses in the local town. They were being held for ransom by the guerrillas. They kept thanking Buck and Rachael for setting them free. Buck began driving again and the road continued to get better until they got on the main road.

When they got to the gas station two hours later, they dropped off their passengers. Buck gave them some U.S. Dollars to help them on their way. Quickly thinking, Rachael told Buck to ask them about any other bad guys and where they were. Upon asking about the location of other bad guys, the two men stopped talking and began thinking, then started talking fast again and motioned to Buck. Rachael grabbed the map and handed it to the two men. They looked at the map and pointed to another place on the map, indicating another mountain on the west side of the lodge. The men talked about seeing big buildings and such.

"How many men were there?" Buck asked.

"Not many," the one man answered in broken English.

Buck thanked them for the information and said goodbye. Before leaving, the two men came up and hugged both Buck and Rachael. Both were crying as they left to go.

"Well, we did our good deed for the day," Buck said as he looked at Rachael.

Rachael, who was tearing up little bit after the encounter, looked at Buck and said, "We done good today."

With that, they headed back to the lodge to enjoy the rest of the day canoeing and snorkeling in the ocean. As Rachael lay sunning herself on the beach later on in the afternoon, Buck came up from the water and sat down next to her in the sand, enjoying the warmth of the sun.

He leaned over and kissed her and she responded with her own kiss to him, saying, "That was nice, I could get used to this."

"Me, too."

Buck lay down next to her and started to doze. They both felt good about the whole day and what they had accomplished. Again getting back late in the evening, they went to the restaurant for dinner and ate out on the patio. The evening was cool and the sounds of the jungle were pleasant to hear. There was a freshness in the air they hadn't noticed before--something similar to a time after the rain had cleaned the air, the freshness and water glistening in the moonlight on the plants and flowers with the Christmas-tree lights glowing to add to the ambiance of the night. For two families, somewhere in Honduras, the night was met with thankfulness and joy, with celebrations that their loved ones were home and safe from the ugly things of the world. Yes, truly, there was happiness in this little part of the world tonight.

The next day Buck and Rachael were up early. When they went down to breakfast, they were met by the same smiling waitress. Seating them next to the fireplace in the nicest part of the restaurant, she took their orders and quickly left. Buck looked around and noticed everyone that was usually here for breakfast was absent. Moreover, Rachael looked at the table they were sitting at and noticed there was a beautiful bouquet of flowers on the table.

Pointing this out to Buck she said, "I wonder what's going on?"

"When the waitress gets back, we'll ask her," He said as he looked around again.

When the waitress came with the food, she was smiling and quite happy. As she placed the plates of food on the table in their respective places, Rachael asked, "Why the flowers and the fireplace?"

"You are one who brought my father back to my family yesterday. We are so thankful you did this for us, my mother wishes she could thank you herself. But she has no way to drive, so I thank you for my mother; you have made her so happy again," the waitress said as she looked at them with tears in her eyes.

"You're more than welcome, glad we could be here to do it," both Buck and Rachael said.

With that, the waitress asked, "Is there anything else I can get for you? I will have your lunches ready for you when you leave today."

Both Buck and Rachael sat there a moment in awe that by doing what they did yesterday would impact someone so close to them and not know it until after the fact. They ate their breakfast silently and quickly, and the lunches were sitting on the counter when they were ready to leave. In fact, the lunches were twice their normal size compared to the first ones they ordered two days earlier.

Buck and Rachael got into their SUV and headed west into the mountains, following the road into the canyon. Using the map, they followed the road until they got to the turnoff. Taking the turnoff from the paved road it soon turned to a dirt road, and after about a mile it turned into a rock trail. The trail was cut out along the side of a mountain just wide enough for one vehicle going in one direction only. The curves were blind and heaven help anybody on the other end of the curve coming around it too fast. Buck intentionally drove slowly, just in case there was other traffic and because it was just easier to do so.

"And I thought California driving was crazy!" Rachael said.

About two miles up the canyon the road opened and they saw a building out in the middle of nowhere, standing alone. Buck backed up the SUV behind the wall of the hill to keep it out of sight. Grabbing his binoculars, he slowly moved forward and surveyed the building and the other smaller building next to it.

He came back and told Rachael, "I see two buildings up there--one real large one and the other quite a bit smaller."

"Did you see anyone up there?"

"No, not a soul."

Buck gave her the binoculars and she took a look for herself.

"So how do you want to proceed?" Buck asked when she got back.

"Why would you have a building out in the middle of nowhere? What are they up to up there?"

"Let's go look."

"So what's the best way to get up there without being seen?"

Buck thought for a moment. "We need to get rid of the SUV--hide it somewhere it can't be seen--and then we can walk up there through the jungle."

Looking at the map again, they saw a trail that led to the top of the mountain, which led into the canyon were the building was. Buck figured they could take the SUV back to the main road and park it in the jungle without it being messed with. With the extra-big lunches and walking, they could be at the building sometime in the evening to check it out. As they made their way back to the main highway, they found a place to hide the SUV and covered it up with some tree limbs to be sure it wouldn't be seen. With their canteens full of water and their backpacks on, they started hiking up the mountain, looking for the trail they saw on the map. The first mile they stayed to the dirt road until they found the trail from the map. At this point they turned left and started up the mountain through the jungle. Fortunately, the trail was easy to follow, although it was rugged. The steepness of the mountain was the hard part for both of them, and the difference in altitude from the lodge was noticeable. Within an hour they were both sweating and out of breath. They decided to stop and take a break and eat their lunches.

"So much for being in good shape," Buck said once he caught his breath.

"You should've stuck to my home cooking instead of letting me off easy by eating out every night."

"Just thinking of you, Dear," Buck smiled. "Did I mention you look beautiful when you're out of breath and the colors of your cheeks are so pretty and red?"

Rachael threw an apple at him and almost hit him with it. "Rats, my aim is off; I think it has something to do with the altitude."

They both laughed and got back up and started on the path again. The climbing started getting easier once they made the ridge on top of the mountain. Once there, Buck used the binoculars again to see where they were in reference to the building. After searching for a couple of minutes, he found the building and realized that it was on the next ridge over from where they were.

With Buck cussing under his breath, Rachael looked up and asked, "What's wrong?"

Buck explained they were one ridge over from where they needed to be. "Oh, is that all? I thought it was worse than that."

"I don't know about you, but I'm tired."

"What happened to that lean, mean fighting machine I married?"

"You're looking at it, Babe. One thing for sure, when we get there it will be dark."

Making up the distance to the other ridge didn't take as long as they had thought. Once on top of the mountain the terrain was easier for hiking. About dusk they made their way down the ridge into the jungle again. This time there was no trail to follow, so they had to depend on the compass Buck carried with him. About 8:00 pm they found the top of a canyon trail they could follow to the building below. Using the moonlight as their light, they were able to make their way down to the building.

Once there, they rested a little while and caught their breath. Buck looked the area over for any signs of people. Not seeing any, they concentrated on looking for booby traps around the buildings. When they didn't see any, they moved from building to building, searching inside each one of them. They heard a low hum coming from the smaller building. It turned out to be a diesel generator used to power the big building. When they checked out the bigger building, they realized they were looking at a big greenhouse with hundreds of poppy plants growing inside, along with cannabis plants. Buck and Rachael figured the structure itself was probably 100 meters long and 40 meters wide, air-conditioned, having a modern irrigation system and other high-tech equipment inside the main building. Buck figured there must be over a thousand poppy plants and that many again in cannabis plants as well. This was amazing to both of them--something this large out in broad daylight and no one being the wiser for it, in a sense hiding in plain sight.

"We need to send a message to Evans about what we've found here," Buck said.

Rachael agreed and pulled out her phone and started to call.

"I'm going to get some pictures of this; no one is going to believe this back home," Buck said.

With that, he went off to get the pictures. Rachael stayed put and called Evans. Within three rings, Evans picked up the phone. "Hello."

"We found what you were looking for," Rachael greeted him.

"Good, where is it?"

Rachael gave him the coordinates according to the map she was looking at.

"Got it," Evans said, as he confirmed it with the GPS from her phone.

"Do you know who's running it?"

"No, not at this time, but Buck is getting pictures of the setup to bring back to show you."

"That's great, well done. We'll see you in a couple of days, Godspeed and good luck."

"Thanks, we'll be there shortly."

About then Buck returned to where Rachael was, "We got company."

With that, both of them went back into the shadows as Buck explained where the men were. They made their way over to where the men were gathered. Buck, using hand signs again, signaled that there were two people in the generator building doing maintenance. Buck and Rachael, staying in the shadows, sat and listened for when they were coming out of the building. As they sat there, the generator stopped and all was quiet. Both buildings went completely dark. They could hear the two men talking to each other. When the generator wouldn't start up, one of the men started cussing in Spanish; after the third try he started getting worried that it wouldn't start at all.

"We may need to call the boss and let him know we're having problems with the generator on the mountain. Pablo isn't going to like this, especially if he has to send somebody from Colombia," He told his partner.

"I think I found the problem," the other mechanic said.

"Try it now," he said after a short pause.

The first mechanic hit the switch to start the generator and it started again, the lights came on inside the green house and the air conditioning started working as well. The two men left the small building and got on their ATVs after putting the tools away and drove down the mountain.

Once they were out of sight, Buck and Rachael made their way down the same trail the two maintenance men took, knowing in the dark it would be quicker and easier to get back to the SUV. Within four hours of following the trail down off the mountain they made their way to the SUV, got in and drove back to the lodge. The sun was starting to come up over the mountains in the east and the birds were singing their typical morning music, acting as a natural alarm clock for the rest of the jungle around the compound. Buck and Rachael were just in time for the morning meal and decided to stop and have breakfast. The same waitress met them with a big smile and asked what they wanted this morning.

Buck looked at Rachael and said, "Let's celebrate our last morning here and have what the waitress suggests."

"What do you suggest we have for breakfast?" Rachael said as she nodded and looked at the waitress.

"I promise you will like what I get for you," The waitress said, smiling.

And then she was gone, yelling to the chef what she wanted ordered for Buck and Rachael. In 15 minutes the food appeared and both were surprised at how much there was to eat.

"So where do we start first?" Buck asked as he looked at the waitress smiling.

The waitress pointed at each plate and said what was on it. She then asked, "Will you a need a lunch today?"

"No, we're leaving today to go back to Miami," Rachael replied.

At this, the waitress frowned and said, "I will miss you when you're gone; please come back soon."

"We will be coming back again soon," Buck reassured her.

"I will be here when you come back." The waitress smiled.

After a short nap Buck and Rachael loaded their clothes into their suitcases and took one last look around the lodge, wishing they could stay longer but anxious to get back to the states. They loaded their SUV with the suitcases and drove to the airport to catch their plane to Miami. They landed in Miami about 6:00 pm and Evans, as usual, was waiting for them. They quickly bypassed customs and made their way to their luggage and were on the road about 45 minutes from touchdown.

"We'll meet in the morning around 9:00 am," Evans said as he took them to their hotel. "Our men will pick you up at 8:45 am."

With that, Evans was gone. Buck and Rachael made their way to the front desk, got their room keys, and went to their room. They got undressed, took a shower, and crawled into bed.

CHAPTER VI

At 7:00the next morning the front desk called room 204 to wake them up. Buck and Rachael were still sound asleep when the call came. The first response Buck had when he heard the cheerful voice on the other end of the phone was to punch whoever it was. The mountain climbing and the late hours had taken their toll on both of them. Rachael was still asleep with the pillow over her head from the phone call.

Buck leaned over to her ear and whispered, "Hey, Beautiful, time to wake up."

At this, she moaned a little and pulled the pillow down over her ears tighter. Buck, seeing this, leaned over again and tickled her feet. At this, she threw the pillow at him, then grabbed his pillow and pulled it over her head. Buck was having fun with this and leaned over again to blow in her ear. This time she hit him with the pillow.

Buck fell onto the floor laughing and Rachael hit him again with the pillow, yelling, "That's for tickling my feet!"

Buck, laughing, crawled over to the bathroom and went in and locked the door.

After about 10 minutes he unlocked the bathroom door. "The shower's ready."

At this, she made her way to the shower as he was shaving. At 8:00 am they went into the dining area and ordered breakfast. By 8:45 both Buck and Rachael were outside waiting for their ride to the federal building. After a couple of minutes the Crown Victoria showed up with the same driver as before. They got into the back of the car and drove to the federal building where Evans and Linda were waiting for them. Everybody was pleased to see each other and as they made their way to the second floor they entered into the communications center.

They stood there as Evans said, "I want to show you something that just came in over the system."

Buck and Rachael watched the monitor that had changed from a map to a regular TV screen. After the picture cleared you could see a white building in the center of the screen with a little building to the side of it.

"Look familiar to you?" Evans asked.

Buck and Rachael guessed it was the buildings they saw in Honduras. Evans said, "Correct; now watch what happens."

Two Honduran helicopters landed with troops and took over the buildings. After two minutes the buildings blew up and caught fire. With the helicopters leaving before the blast, nobody was hurt in the operation and two people were arrested.

"The report from the Honduran army said that 1000 poppy plants and 800cannabis plants were destroyed in the fire and explosion. A new era of the drug war has hit Honduras and now it has the attention of DEA, Customs, and Immigration and Customs Enforcement (ICE). Oh, by the way, the Honduran government wanted to thank you for getting those hostages released. The army tracked down the guerillas and captured all of them, and now they're sitting in jail waiting for a trial," Evans said.

"Well, the town wasn't big enough for both of us, so we did what we had to do," Buck said as he looked at Evans.

They laughed at this and left the communications center and headed to Evans' office.

After closing the door to his office Evans asked, "Tell me all of the gory details of your trip and don't spare anything."

Buck and Rachael explained how they were able to find the greenhouse with the help of the two men they had rescued and what they had learned from listening to the maintenance men working on the generator about a guy named Pablo from Colombia. Evans got excited about this and looked at Linda when the name came up and Linda, smiling, nodded her head as Evans looked at her.

"Are you sure the two guys said Pablo for the one that would be upset from Colombia?" Evans asked.

Buck and Rachael, sensing this was important to Evans and Linda, said, "Yes, most definitely."

"We finally got him," Evans said as he smiled at Linda.

"It's almost too good to be true," Linda replied.

Buck and Rachael looked at each other, not understanding the importance of what they had said.

"Who is this Pablo?" Buck asked.

"Forgive us for keeping you guessing about this. We, which is our government, have been looking for the biggest drug kingpin for years, and so far up to this point we've been unable to find him. This Pablo, also known as the "Boss," is supposedly based in Mexico. However, that being said, he moves from place to place to keep from being caught. Every attempt to capture him has been foiled because he's very good at hiding and also because of the leak we have in our organization," Evans said, looking at Buck and Rachael.

"If what the maintenance men said is true, and with nobody else knowing, we can send a team to go get him," Linda said.

"We're not talking about Martinez, are we?" Rachael said, looking at both Evans and Linda.

"Yes, we are," Linda and Evans said, smiling at her.

She sat there for a moment, stunned by their answer, and Buck looked at all of them, asking, "Care to fill me in on this Martinez?"

Rachael apologized to Buck saying, "Remember when we worked together in Arizona trying to find Jim and his connection to the drugs? Well, we figured he was connected to the Monterrey Cartel. Remember we couldn't make that connection because we never caught Jim."

"And now we have that connection because of the two maintenance men?" Buck asked.

Rachael shook her head yes. "We all had the impression he was the big drug connection into the United States, but with no one talking we couldn't prove it, plus on top of that we couldn't find him. With just the four of us knowing or having an idea of where he is, we can concentrate our efforts in Colombia and maybe finally capture him."

"From our last phone call with you guys Rachael said you took pictures of the place while you were there," Evans stated.

"Yes, I did," Buck replied.

Reaching into his pocket, Buck handed the S-drive disc over to Evans, and Rachael said, "We didn't develop them yet simply because we weren't sure we could get it done fast enough before we left."

Evans called his secretary into the office and handed the disc over to her. "Please get these photos developed as fast as you can."

The secretary took the disc and headed out the door. Buck went on to say, "I found this symbol of Obama Care written over two revolvers facing each other."

Evans thought for a minute. "Linda, don't we have a book with all of the symbols and markings on the drugs we have intercepted over the years?"

"Yes, it's down in the library on the first floor." Linda said.

"We'll bring it up for you to peruse at your leisure." Evans said.

When the brief was over it was time for lunch and they all headed out to a place called Doug's Genuine Food and Drink restaurant for a bite to eat.

"Have you any leads in the leak situation?" Buck asked while eating.

"No, not yet. We believe it's someone on the inside of our agency. It could be an agent or maybe a staff member working in support; we just don't know," Evans said.

"We've lost a group of court cases because the information was compromised before we even got to court. All we know for sure is every move we make the bad guys already know about it before we even make it, thus wasting our time and money on cases that were supposedly slam dunk," Linda added.

"What happens now that we're back?" asked Rachael.

"Well, now that you are back from your honeymoon and you're here…" He stopped a moment and looked at Linda to read her face. Linda looked back and nodded to him. Evans continued, "…we were wondering if you would like to stay a couple more days and help us find our leak?"

"What would it entail?" Buck said as he looked at Rachael.

"We have a few leads for who we think it might be, but not for certain. We would like you to be our private eyes and do some digging around for us. We'll be acting as if you're going with us to Colombia and will give you the training updates and Intel on the case. Your job will be to find out who it is. The Intel we give you will be bogus but believable for our use in ferreting out the leak. Mind you, this could be dangerous if they find out you are in on the hunt. Well, what do you say?" Evans asked.

"Do we stay in the hotel we're in?" Rachael asked Evans, who nodded yes to her question.

"Maybe I'll finally get my suntan," Rachael said to Buck.

"Your dime, our time," Buck said.

"What we think is somebody's looking at our e-mail traffic and following our every move from a distance. We think that someone is sending the coded e-mail traffic to another place in the building and using it as a jumping off point to South America," Evans stated.

"Have you run a diagnostics on your software systems yet?" Buck asked.

"Yes, we have, but we haven't found anything out of order. Whoever is doing this is good, really good," Linda replied.

"We figure you guys are outside the normal food chain and you might pick something up we missed. This is what we have so far," Evans said.

Reaching into his briefcase, Evans pulled out a file and handed it to Rachael. "You will understand the FBI jargon better than Buck, so you can explain it to him better than him trying to make sense of it all and losing time."

"How much time do we have on this?" Rachael asked.

"Knowing how fast you two work, I'd say you'll need a few days to figurc it out. However, we are planning the move into Colombia in about two weeks, maybe less. We need to look as if it's business as usual without raising suspicions. You two will be able to move freely after the training to enjoy Miami and the good life here," Evans replied.

Rachael looked over the file and was surprised to see Evans' secretary on the list of possible source leaks and asked, "Have you run background checks on all of these people?"

"Yes, that's why these names came up. Nothing major was found, but there were some peculiarities, nothing that would indicate major issues but still odd little things," Evans replied. "Well, Linda and I need to get back to the office for the daily grind. We can drop you off at your hotel so you can get yourselves a car, and we'll see you tomorrow for the first part of your training." Again reaching into his briefcase, Evans pulled something out. "Oh, by the way, here are badges for you to use while you're down here."

After being dropped off at the hotel, Buck and Rachael headed to their room, sat down and started reading the file Evans had given them. There were three names on the list, one of which was the secretary. Her name was Mary Dominguez. She had been working as a secretary for six years and had no really outstanding issues in her record to indicate anything out of the ordinary. The next name was Mike Hunt, who was a computer specialist. He had been hired two years ago as an intern and was lucky enough to be able to stay on after his internship was over. His record showed he had a computer-science degree from Florida State University with a minor in criminal justice. His personnel records indicated some small incidents while in college-- nothing major--more like college pranks than any real issues per se. The third person was the janitor whose name was George Rasmussen. George had been working as a janitor for approximately 10 years and was a U.S. Army retiree. No record at all other than yearly evaluations indicating a good worker. As Rachael finished reading the material, they started thinking about what-if scenarios that would cause these three to turn on their country.

"Let's follow the secretary first; I'm feeling lucky on this one," Buck said.

Rachael thought for a moment. "She doesn't get off work until later this afternoon. Let's go check her place and see what turns up. Then we can drive by and look at the other places where the other two live, as well."

Buck agreed to the plan and went about getting a rental car to use.

When the car arrived, Buck signed all of the paperwork necessary to take it. In the meantime, Rachael used the computer in the computer room to look up the addresses of the three people and try to figure out the best route to go and in what order to hit all of them in minimum time.

After some minutes of getting oriented on the map, the closest place was Mike Hunt's address. With that, they headed down the road looking for Mike's place. After turning on the street where Mike lived, they drove to his place and stopped outside his house and just looked it over. Nothing out of the ordinary appeared to them.

"Let's get out and look around," Rachael said.

Buck and Rachael moved around the house looking in the windows to see inside. There was nothing in the backyard that would indicate anything out of the ordinary. The inside of the house didn't have expensive furniture; in fact, it looked like a bachelor's pad, nothing other than what you would expect to find in a place being lived in by a group of guys. When they returned to the car, they got in and drove away.

"If he's making money by selling secrets, he must have the money somewhere else," Rachael said.

"The house reminds me of my old college days."

"One down, two to go."

The next place they drove to was the secretary's place. It was a first-floor apartment in a quiet neighborhood. They were able to get in the apartment without being seen. As they went in, they checked out her bedroom and other areas, making sure they didn't disturb anything that would indicate that they had been there. When searching her mail, they found a letter from a family member that was living in Colombia.

Rachael called Buck, "I think I've found something that might interest you."

Buck came into the kitchen and saw the letter Rachael was holding and asked, "What does it say?"

Rachael read the letter aloud. "Your parents are doing fine and all is well for them. They are looking forward to returning home once you send the information that you promised. Remember, tell no one about what you're doing."

"What information are they talking about?" Buck asked.

Rachael looked at Buck, wondering the same thing. Putting the letter and envelope in Buck's pocket, they looked for more letters like this and found in her nightstand several letters from the same area. The first letter she received was from a family member detailing the parents being taken and held someplace not identified by known cartel people, stipulating that they would be all right if she would get specific information dealing with what the FBI had on the Monterrey Cartel.

Buck read the letter aloud to Rachael, "I think we found our leak."

"That poor girl; her parents are being used by the cartel to get information to keep ahead of the FBI. I wonder if her parents are even still alive," Rachael said.

With letters in their hands they exited the apartment, careful not to be seen. Once back in the car, they headed to George Rasmussen's place. As they parked the car, they noticed that there were kids running in and out of the front door.

Rachael looked at Buck, "Well, how do we check this place out?"

Buck sat there a moment, "Just wait; knowing any family, she'll need to go to the store eventually."

After an hour of sitting, the wife came out with the kids and loaded them up into the van and drove off. Buck, seeing this, said, "That's our cue."

They got out of the car and walked over to the house. Rachael took the backyard and started looking around the area. Buck looked inside the windows and saw a typical house with a family living in it. Toys were strewn all over the place. The kitchen looked like a tornado had ripped through it; in other words, it looked normal for a family with small children. Rachael called out to Buck, asking him to come here.

When Buck got there he asked, "What's up?"

Rachael showed him the paper she had found in the trash and handed it to him. As Buck looked at it, he realized it had been marked classified and the wording on the paper indicated information that dealt with operations in Nicaragua.

"Well, well, well, what do we have here?"

"Maybe we have two moles."

With this information and the letters, they headed back to the federal building. On the way there they contacted Evans and told him what they had found.

"Don't come back here; I'll meet you at the same restaurant where we had lunch," Evans told them.

After Rachael closed out the call, she told Buck, "Head to the restaurant where we had lunch."

After being seated, they waited about 15 minutes for Evans and Linda to show up. As they sat down at the table, Buck pulled out the letters from the secretary and the classified material from the trash at Rasmussen's home. As Evans and Linda looked at the letters and classified stuff that Buck and Rachael found, they sat back in their chairs and let out a moan of frustration.

"How could I be so blind? Their background checks never indicated anything like this was going on," Evans thought to himself out loud.

"At least we caught them. Now what do we do with them?" Linda asked, looking at Evans.

"Take them out and shoot them," Evans answered quickly.

"I think your secretary was under duress as they were using her parents as leverage to get the information they wanted. As far as Rasmussen goes, I don't know about him," Rachael said.

"Why don't we use them for our purposes?" Buck asked.

Evans and Linda looked at him, thinking about what he said. Evans looked at Linda. "Do we have anything that would work for us like that?"

Linda thought a minute and said, "How about we set them up so we catch them red-handed passing information? Maybe they could lead us to the kingpin and his location or where the poppy farms are. The first thing to do is evaluate the damage they've done and go from there to turn it around."

"How about we set up a raid in Colombia at a certain location and then feed the secretary the wrong location to throw them off and catch them when they're moving?" Rachael asked.

With that thought in mind, the group of them started thinking about the scenarios they could play out that would be almost true yet completely misleading, without the secretary or the janitor catching on.

"How about we go after the kingpin by trying to burn all of his poppy farms in Colombia? This would bring him out of hiding and would force his people to come out and defend the poppy farms. We could monitor the radio traffic and follow the sources of the radio signals back to our drug kingpin," Buck said.

"We could pretend that the Colombian army decides to do a big combined joint strike with DEA with a massive sweep across a certain area that we know has the poppy farms, and then pretend to feed the information to everyone that would be involved, the Colombian army and DEA. But it's all false. We post all of this information through meetings here in the Miami office and let the false information leak out to the bad guys via our moles. They in turn pass this information on to their connections in the cartel," Rachael added.

"How would we track the information being leaked out?" Evans asked.

"We put a type of tracking software in the e-mails and watch where they go. Who can we trust to do this in the Information Technology (IT) section without blowing the mission?" Linda asked.

"Our IT guys could plant an app on the secretary's computer that allows us to see her e-mail traffic, no matter what computers she's on. By tracking her e-mails they should lead us to the big guy in charge," Evans said.

"By following the e-mail traffic we can follow the specific e-mail to wherever it goes, like the Colombian army or DEA. This way we find the leaks in the Colombian army and possibly other leaks as well along the e-mail chain," Buck said.

"Maybe we could plant a virus in the e-mail, as well, to screw up their computer-network system--a virus that would allow us to track their every move without them knowing it, maybe affect their computers to disrupt their business. The real question is, is it feasible to plant a virus or a Trojan horse into their system?" Rachael asked.

"I'm sure if we ask the right organization in the Intel alphabet world they probably already have one that works," Buck said.

Evans thought for a moment and said, "Linda, do we have connections in the Counterintelligence Agency (CIA) or maybe National Security Agency (NSA) who could help us with this?"

"Let me look into it and I'll let you know," Linda replied.

"Then it's agreed that we will play this out to trap the moles but also, hopefully, the kingpin as well. All we need is the computer savvy to set up the spyware and virus on the secretary's computer and let it run its course. Buck, Rachael, we'll need you to be in on the planning of the mission into Columbia and work with our people who are familiar with where the poppy farms are," Evans said as he closed the meeting.

Buck and Rachael nodded in agreement. "What is the timeline on this?"

"One week, maybe two at the most. In the meantime we will do a thorough background check on our two leaks to figure out what the damage is and how to contain it. Linda, as you said, follow up with the Intel arena and see if there is a certain type of bug or code we can use to follow the e-mail traffic that is transparent to everybody, except us. Is there anything else or anyone else who needs to be brought in on this?" Evans asked.

They all looked around and said, "No, not at this time."

"One final thought: We should use a safe place to meet from now on until we figure it's safe in the building," Evans said.

"Should we have a code word to let everyone know about needing to meet?" asked Linda.

Rachael looked at everybody sitting there and said, "I've got one; let's use the word VACATION as the code word."

Everybody laughed and Buck said, "Works for me."

Everybody agreed; with that, they all got up from the table and left to go do their part of the mission. Buck and Rachael followed

Evans and Linda back to the federal building to meet with the others that would facilitate them in their part of the plan.

Evans introduced Buck and Rachael to Bill Art and Cathy Smith and told them they would be working with Buck and Rachael to plan an operation to go after the poppy fields in Columbia, South America.

Linda called security and asked them to start background checks on all of the support staff working in the building but to do it quietly and report back to her or to Evans when they were done. Linda then went to her Rolodex, which she kept under lock and key in her desk, and started going through the names of who might be helpful in setting up a transparent spyware for the FBI. After skimming through the names, she came across a onetime acquaintance she had met while in Quantico going through some refresher training. Adam Finch, who worked at NSA as a field agent, had come from the Baltimore office to learn better shooting skills at Quantico. They had hit it off after the classes were over for the day and became chummy during their stay there in Virginia. Linda contacted Adam Finch, and after explaining their need of a transparent spyware that could only be seen by their organization, he said he would look into it.

Evans contacted the IT people and asked them to do a check on the staff's computers to determine the routing of e-mails and where they went. Specifically, e-mail traffic being sent to e-mail addresses like home, out-of-state, etc. The IT people claimed that they could track any e-mails originating from the federal building to anywhere. Evans challenged the IT team to find the e-mail/user that had sent an e-mail to the farthest destination. He told them they had two days to accomplish this, and as a reward for their hard work, he would give the team their choice of a Monday or Friday off work. The team took the challenge and proceeded with fervor.

CHAPTER VII

With everybody doing their part the table was set and now it became a waiting game. Buck and Rachael were looking at two sets of satellite photos taken of Colombia. The infrared photos showed what appeared to be hot spots all through the jungle. These hot spots were compared to normal satellite photos where the jungle appeared; chances are they were cooking farms. These places were marked as possible sites with GPS coordinates. Rachael did the listing of the possible sites and was searching any other satellite photos for confirmation of these sites of interest. The only real solution for verification would be to have boots on the ground to look. That being said, it was time consuming and costly in manpower and equipment.

Bill and Cathy had been very helpful in identifying anything out of the ordinary. Both had spent time in the military doing imagery analysis, having been trained at Good fellow Air Force Base in Texas. After their enlistment was up they worked as contractors for NSA until they went to work for the FBI. For them it was a challenge to find something unusual or out of place. Both were good at finding the hot spots in Colombia. In about three hours they had 10 possible sites within a 30-mile radius of a village called St. Lucia. As with all probable sites, it was always a gamble as to if it was real or not. With these sites listed they sent a request for confirmation to the NSA and CIA imagery section. Sometimes the different angle of the satellite taking the picture would show something more than the overhead pictures. Of course, this would take time for all of the players to participate. Fortunately, Bill and Cathy had made friends with their counterparts, thereby shaving the timelines for quicker assessments. What would normally take weeks to review could be accomplished in hours. It might cost them a case of beer; a few steaks or others favors asked of them. Bill and Cathy were always ready and willing to accommodate the needs of their friends in the imagery world.

Linda walked into Evans office with the list of the possible sites and with a message from Adam Finch about the software that they could use for transparent spyware. After making a quick check with the IT people, Evans found that thcy could create the same spyware that would work better than the one Adam had suggested. It would only take a day to generate and a lot less paperwork. With that, Evans gave the IT team the go-ahead to build it.

Buck and Rachael went to Evans office to say goodnight and that they were on their way back to the hotel to get some rest for the next day.

"Thank you for your input and ideas today," Evans said.

"'tweren't nothing, mister; we're just doing our jobs," Buck replied.

Rachael and Evans laughed and both said, "Goodnight, we'll see you tomorrow."

Buck and Rachael walked to where their car was parked, and as they were getting into it, they noticed Rasmussen heading to his car as well.

"Well, what do you think?" Buck said, looking at Rachael.

"Let's follow him and if he goes home, we'll head back to the hotel."

Rasmussen pulled out of the parking lot and turned into the right lane with Buck and Rachael following about two car lengths behind.

"Do you remember his home address?" Buck asked Rachael.

"Yes, I do, and this isn't the way to his home."

As they followed him, they realized that they were going into a park. Buck kept looking for an address so that he could tell Evans about the location. Rachael caught the sign identifying the park as Oleta River

State Park. With that, they concentrated on following Rasmussen. He ended up parking near a picnic area where you could sit on benches and watch the river. As Rasmussen got out of his car, he went to one of the benches and sat down. Buck and Rachael pulled up into a parking spot nearby and waited to see what would happen next.

In about 10 minutes another car pulled into the parking lot next to where Rasmussen had parked. The man in the car got out and walked over to where Rasmussen was sitting and sat down on the other side of the bench. After looking around, the man handed Rasmussen an envelope and Rasmussen handed him some paperwork. They both got up and left, going in different directions. While sitting there, Buck was watching everything while Rachael copied the license plate of the car and wrote down the description of the man.

Rasmussen was the first to leave the state park, and after five more minutes the man got into his car and drove off as well. Buck started the engine in their car and pulled out of his parking spot and followed the man in his car. After leaving North Miami Beach, the man pulled onto Interstate 95, heading north. They followed the car up to Pompano Beach city. Then they proceeded to take the exit to the Pompano Beach airport and followed him into the flight operations center. The man walked out of the flight operations center and boarded a waiting Lear Jet, which then taxied out to the runway and took off.

Buck and Rachael walked into the flight operations center and after showing their badges asked the flight dispatcher who was on the plane. The flight dispatcher said it was a corporate jet that belonged to a company in South America. Rachael asked the dispatcher if they had a flight plan for the plane. The flight dispatcher looked at the flight manifest and said it's flying to Bogota', Colombia, South America, via Mexico City.

"Does it list the company the plane was registered to?" Buck asked.

"No."

With the information from the flight dispatcher and a copy of the flight plan, they made their way back to the car and drove to Miami. Rachael called Evans and said, "We need to talk about our vacation time; when can we meet?"

Looking at his watch, Evans noticed it was 7:30 pm. "Where are you now?"

Rachael looked for the signs from the interstate. "We are on I-95, heading south back to Miami; we just passed the turnoff to Fort Lauderdale."

"We'll see you at our apartment in about a half hour, and we'll put some coffee on for when you get here," Evans said.

At about 8:30 pm Buck and Rachael rang the doorbell and waited for the door to open. Rachael looked at Buck, smiling. "All I wanted to do was have a nice quiet dinner and stay home and watch some TV, but, no, you decided we needed some nightlife in another town. See what you've started."

"You're killing me, Smalls," Buck said as he looked at Rachael and chuckled to himself.

Evans opened the door. "Come on in and sit down on the couch. Linda will be out shortly."

When Linda came out, she sat down next to Evans and listened to what Buck and Rachael had to say. Rachael said, "We were on our way out of the building earlier when we noticed Rasmussen walking out of the building to his car. We decided to follow him to see where he went.

"Like we had nothing else to do tonight," Buck interjected.

Rachael smiled and continued speaking. "We thought we would follow him to see where he was headed; if straight home, we would call it a day ourselves, and if not, we would see where he went."

"He went to a park called Oleta River State Park and sat down on a bench. After about five minutes this guy showed up and an exchange was made between the two of them. Then, after about five minutes, they both left. We followed the guy in the car, who had taken the paperwork to Pompano airport, and watched him fly out on a Lear Jet," Buck said.

Rachael proceeded to tell Evans and Linda about the description of the man and the car he was driving. "The man was about 6 feet tall, 200 pounds, dark hair, with a mustache. The car was a 2016 white Ford Lincoln, four doors, with a vanity license plate saying "Dustman."

Evans asked Rachael for her notes. "In the morning we'll look this information up and process it, anything else?"

"But wait; there's more," Buck chimed in.

"As you know, we followed the white Ford Lincoln to the Pompano airport. When the plane took off, we went into the flight operations center and talked to the dispatcher, who kindly gave us a copy of the flight plan, where the plane was from and where it was going," Rachael said.

With that, they handed the flight-plan information over to Linda and said, smiling, "Can we go home now, Boss?"

Evans and Linda smiled at the question, and Evans said, "Take the rest of the night off and we'll see you in the morning; maybe we'll have some information for you about the car and the flight plan when you come in."

"Remember when we had a place in Arizona and we were complaining that it was too quiet and that we were bored of the quiet nights and slow mornings?" Rachael said to Buck. "Well, I take it all back. Your friends here like living on the edge of adventure and fun, and I'm getting too old for this kid stuff anymore."

They all laughed, and this time with a smile Evans said, "Get out of here before I change my mind and make you stay out all night."

With that, they said their goodnights and drove back to their hotel. Evans looked at Linda as Buck and Rachael left their place and said, "Man oh man, what's happening here?"

"We need to contact the next level up and let them know what's going on down here."

"Only after we clean this up."

"I agree; otherwise, we're going to look pretty silly about all of this."

Buck and Rachael finally got back to their hotel about 11:00 pm. Both were tired and ready for bed when they got to their room. Rachael looked at Buck and said, "You sure know how to show a girl a good time."

"Should we go and get something to eat while we're still standing?" Buck laughed.

"You always say the right things."

As they walked down to the restaurant holding hands, they made their way to a booth and sat down. The waitress came over and took their order. Sitting there for a moment saying nothing, just being there together, Buck looked over at Rachael. "I love you. I can't think of anybody else that I would rather be doing all of this crazy stuff with than you."

"I love you too, Sweetheart."

After they finished eating they went to their room, got undressed and fell asleep holding each other.

The next morning came way too early for Buck and Rachael to suit their needs, still trying to recover from the night before. The phone in the hotel room was ringing and Rachael answered the phone. "Hello, this had better be important."

The voice on the other end stammered a little bit before saying why they had called. It was the secretary from Evans' office telling them to meet at the same restaurant at 11:30 for lunch. Rachael was happy about not having to go to the federal building and hung up the hotel phone and went back to sleep.

At 11:30 Buck and Rachael were there at the restaurant, sitting at a table waiting when Evans and Linda walked in. Buck motioned for them and they walked over and sat down.

"So how goes the battle at the office?" Buck asked.

Evans smiled and Linda rolled her eyes at the question. Both Buck and Rachael could tell that Linda and Evans were not in a good mood. Both of them sat and waited for Evans to say something. After a minute or two Evans finally spoke, saying, "Well it's like this: The car is registered to a Michael Nunez, a Colombian national who works for a company here in Miami named Maxwell Development Corporation. We did a trace on the company and found that its parent company is based in Bogota', Colombia, and is called San Juan Enterprises and has extensive reach into everything that has to do with money. With some further checking we found that the president and owner of the corporation is a known money launderer for the cartels in México. He owns banks, has land holdings and other businesses all over South America; he's worth approximately, conservatively speaking, 300 million dollars."

"So how does Rasmussen fit into all of this?" Buck asked.

"After digging a little deeper into his background, we found out he had spent some time down in Colombia as an Army Special Forces trainer to the Colombian army in combat tactics and electronic equipment, which included listening devices. We figure something happened down there that he either got hooked on the money from the cartel or was somehow blackmailed. No matter what it was, he has been working with the cartel since he was hired here and with his access to the building he knew everything that was going on, all of it. One more thing: After we checked on his finances, we found Rasmussen had two different savings accounts, one for his normal life to include his retirement pay and money he gets from being a janitor at the federal building. The other offshore account was set up under a false name and has money coming in from overseas, probably South America and has about 500 thousand dollars in it. We are still trying to trace where the money is coming from, but no luck as of yet," Linda said.

"Since finding this out, we have gone through every room in the federal building with an electronic bug detector and found one in my office, one inside the communications center and one more in Linda's office. These bugs are the passive kind; in other words, they don't activate until someone is talking. The only way we found them was by having a fake meeting, which activated the bugs. These bugs are very sophisticated electronic listening devices; only the Special Forces and the CIA have these kinds of bugs available," Evans said.

Rachael and Buck sat and listened to Linda and Evans and thought about all of the conversations about classified information that were now compromised because of the bugs in the offices.

"After thinking about it some more, we want to continue with our plan of drawing out the kingpin, except now it's for real. The cartel has made fools of us for the last time. I want this SOB bad, real bad," Evans said.

"We've left the bugs in place so as not to tip our hands, and all our meetings will constitute giving out false information to track down this kingpin," Linda said.

"What about the secretary and her role as a leak?" Rachael asked.

"We found out that her parents are being held in one of the cartels' safe houses in Bogota'. When we confronted her about the letters she received from her parents, she broke down in tears. She had wanted to come forward but didn't know how to go about it without alerting the cartel. Her damage was minimal but the damage was still done; however, she has agreed to assist us in giving out some misinformation to start the ball rolling," Linda answered.

"So where do we start?" Buck asked.

"It already has started. We will continue using the satellite photos as a way of tracking the farms, and we will use the Colombian army to do the footwork for us. That way they will get all of the credit and it will help the president look good politically to his people. As far as a code name for this operation, we came up with the name of Judas. We think that it's an appropriate name for this situation," Evans replied.

Buck and Rachael had never seen Evans this upset before. That being said, they knew why and knew he was after blood on this one and really didn't care about the fallout. Linda was just as determined as Evans was and ready to play the game to the fullest extent necessary.

Buck tried to lighten the mood by saying, "You know, I kind of feel sorry for the bad guys, and I really don't think they realize what they've done."

"They will shortly after we hand them their asses on a plate," Evans said.

Linda looked around, "Shall we order lunch now?"

As they ate their lunches, they talked about what the next steps would be to keep the ball rolling in operation Judas. They needed eyes on the ground that they could trust in finding the kingpin. This time the eyes on the ground would have backup from some professional people. Special Operations had been requested to be used in this part of the plan; that is, they were to go in and get the kingpin, release the parents of the secretary, and destroy the safe house along the way. Timing was the issue; everything had to happen at the right time for this to be successful.

After talking the plan out with Buck and Rachael, Evans asked, "I need to ask you a favor and if you say no we will understand. Linda and I have decided to ask you guys to go to Colombia to work with Special

Operations to go in and get the kingpin and the parents."

Buck and Rachael sat there surprised; not knowing what to say, they just sat there for a moment. Buck asked first, "What would we be doing there?"

"You guys would be acting again as a couple on vacation and would be scouting the area looking for the safe house. The other team would be working with the Colombian army going after the farms. That would be their cover story, but in all actuality, they would be looking for the kingpin. You guys would be their eyes and ears doing the legwork. Once you find the safe house they would come in and get the parents out. Your other job would be to try and locate where the kingpin is hiding so that the team could go in and get him," Evans replied.

"This is the tricky part for you and probably the most dangerous, as well. If you two get found out, it could have a bad outcome for you both," Linda added.

Rachael turned and looked at Buck for a minute, waiting for his reply. Buck looked at Evans and Linda, then back at Rachael, and said, "Oh, sure, work for the FBI and see the world."

They all took that as a yes and laughed for the first time in a long time. With that, the real training began for Buck and Rachael. Evans told them to meet Linda in her office starting tomorrow morning at 8:00 am. From there she would take them to where they needed to go. After Evans and Linda left to go back to work, Buck and Rachael sat there for a little while thinking about everything that had gone on.

"They really need our help to pull this off," Buck said, looking at Rachael.

"Wow, who would have thought all this stuff was happening right under their noses. Leastwise, when our kids ask us what we did for fun, we can say if we told you, we would have to shoot you."

They both laughed at this and got up to go to their car. The drive back to the hotel was a quiet drive. Once there they changed their clothes and got their swimming suits on and found the nearest beach and laid in the sun to work on their suntans.

Lying in the sun, Rachael reached over and took Buck's hand and held it saying, "You know I love you?"

"Where else can I have a paid vacation and see the world with a beautiful lady next to me?"

They laughed and dozed in the sun, knowing that this might be the last time they would get the chance to relax and enjoy the good life for a while. Buck opened his eyes, leaned over and kissed Rachael on the cheek and closed his eyes once more. Rachael smiled and moved closer to Buck.

CHAPTER VIII

The next morning was as beautiful as could be expected when you're in paradise. The air was sweet with the smell of orange trees in bloom and the sea breeze coming in from the ocean. The sunrise caught both Rachael and Buck still in bed. Rachael woke up first, started the coffee and started getting ready for the day. After the coffee was ready Rachael woke Buck up by tickling his ear. Buck started to move away from the tickle and almost fell out of bed. By then he was awake and yawning, looking for his first cup of coffee, which Rachael had in her hand waiting for him. After sitting up on the bed, he reached for the coffee and cradled it in his hands for a second and slowly took a sip of it to start the day. Buck's eyes were wide open now, and as he made his way to the bathroom to take a shower, Rachael started cooking some breakfast in the small kitchen.

Both Buck and Rachael were in Linda's office by 7:55 am and were waiting for her. She soon arrived and apologized for being late. "A meeting came up and couldn't be avoided."

"I think she forgot we are on vacation and don't have a time schedule yet," Buck said as he smiled at her.

Linda laughed and pointing to the clock where they found the bug. "Oh yeah, rub it in."

With that, Linda motioned them to come outside the office, saying, "So tell me where you vacationers went yesterday?"

Once clear of her office, Linda started talking about the schedule she had for Buck and Rachael today. "Once you get your brief about the country, your next meeting will consist of learning some of the language and, last of all, our contacts down there that may be of help to you."

"What about the cavalry being down there?" Buck asked.

"You two will be flying down there with them; they have a mission with the local army there first. They connect with you at a place called Parque de la 93. It's in the nice part of Bogota' and, as tourists, you'll be fine there. After that you will follow the team into the place where the safe house is. Rescue the family there and leave without a trace."

"Sounds as if you know where the safe house is," Rachael said.

Linda replied, "We have been following some Signals Intelligence (SigInt) information from Fort Huachuca, and they have narrowed it down to this one neighborhood called Kennedy. It's not considered a dangerous neighborhood, but you should be careful looking around, just the same."

"I owe the IT gang a day off for their hard work; they found the e-mail address and location of the safe house, leastwise within a block or two. And, to top it off, they were able to plant a virus on the computer that we can track with our own electronic gear, kind of like a homing signal," Evans said as he walked into the conversation.

"Good news for our side," Linda said.

With that, Linda took them to their first training class and introduced them to Betty, who would be their instructor. "Treat them good and make sure they learn all that they need to know about Bogota' and anything else that is pertinent."

After Linda left, Betty introduced herself again. "I'm Betty and just to let you know my background, I've spent sixteen months in Colombia on a mission for the LDS church and married a guy I met there while serving. We lived there for another 10 years and finally moved to the U.S. about two years ago for our children."

She proceeded to tell Buck and Rachael about Bogota' and about Colombia. "Most of the information you're about to hear comes from Wikivoyage and Trip Advisor, so if you want to know more, you'll have an idea of where to look for it. Bogota' has a population of about 10 million people. It's the capital and is the largest city of Colombia. Bogota' is located in the center of the country in the eastern part of the Andes Mountains. The city is one of the capitals with the highest elevation at 8,530 ft., so you'll need to dress warm at night. Here is a map of Bogota'; you need to study it carefully. You'll notice that the streets and avenues are named Carreras (Avenues) and Calles (Streets), which run perpendicular to one another, with a few exceptions. Once you learn their street system you will find it easier to move around."

With Buck and Rachael looking at the map, Betty had the two run a few addresses down to make sure they understood what she had told them. After 15 minutes of finding addresses Buck and Rachael felt comfortable moving about the neighborhood.

"There are a few things you need to remember about Bogota'. First, many streets do not have "Walk/Don't Walk" signs. Therefore, you have to be very careful and look every which way before crossing the street, especially when you get to the roundabouts. Second, motorcycles do not always follow the same rules as the other cars. They act more like cyclists in the fact that they may run a red light if they see no cars are coming from the perpendicular street ahead of them. Stay alert, and be extra cautious for them. Third, when walking down the street, you should always check the street number you are on. Sometimes the Carrera or Calle will change, even though you have not switched streets."

At this point Betty moved on to the neighborhood setup. "Bogotá is divided into four sections: The South is mainly the poorer section of the city. El Centro, which translates "Center," is the city's original downtown and hosts most of its traditional heritage locations, city and public offices and financial headquarters. El Occidente, is home to Bogotá's major sporting venues and outdoor parks, as well as residence areas for main middle- and some upper-class living. The last section is the North, which is where most modern development has taken place. This section combines many upscale living spaces with affluent shopping centers, boutiques, cafes, nightclubs, and many new business neighborhoods, which offer headquarters to many multinational corporations."

"I think this is where the company San Juan Enterprises is located," Buck said, leaning over to Rachael.

"You would be correct," Betty replied.

"The principal safety concerns for travelers are muggings and taxi crime." She continued, "Muggers are usually high on drugs and armed with knives or guns, and you should simply give them what they ask for without a fight—it's never anything worth dying over. Neighborhoods that are frequented by travelers that have a significant problem with muggings include La Candelaria, most parts of Santa Fé, and to a much lesser extent, the more southern parts of Chapinero close to Avenida Caracas. The muggings usually occur after dark on weeknights; daytime walks and Friday and Saturday nights are fine. Los Mártires is a place to be on guard any time of day."

"The taxi crime is a weird problem there. While longer-term visitors will find themselves lazily hailing cabs now and then, it is best to call cabs and not hail them off the street. Any cab dispatched will be safe, while hailed cabs are infrequent, but a little too frequent for comfort and are considered dangerous. It may take a bit longer, but your safety is worth an extra wait. Hotels and nicer restaurants will always be happy to call one for you. Oh, one more thing to watch out for is the Million Dollar Ride. It happens often enough in most social situations with the locals; at least someone or someone close to them has had the experience. It occurs when you hail a taxi on the street, the taxi stops, you get in, then someone else gets in with you; and they take you for a ride until you have taken an important sum out of your bank accounts. This is usually accomplished with legitimate threats of violence."

Betty also cautioned them about ATM muggings. She advised, "Pay attention when using cash machines that nobody follows you after you have withdrawn the money. It's a precaution foreign visitors aren't always used to taking, but it's not hard— look around as you step up to the machine to see if anyone's paying too much attention, then do the same afterwards. If someone is, abort and/or go into a store or eatery and stay put. Try to use ATMs that are inside the supermarket--Éxito always has them--while still paying attention to your surroundings."

Sounds like New York after dark most nights," Rachael said.

"True, the problem with Bogota'is there is no one you can call if you get caught in a jam down there," Betty replied.

With her part of the briefing done, another trainer was waiting in the back of the room. He was there to teach them a few words of Spanish to assist them in their travels. With living in Arizona and with the population in Smith County being split half English and half Spanish, this part of the training was simple.

The last bit of training they received was done by Betty again. She reintroduced herself, saying, "Having lived in Colombia for almost half of my adult life, I have learned that this is a city where no one trusts one another or tries to help one another very much. The general attitude towards the criminals is that there's little to be done about them, so the best course of action is just to avoid trouble. And the best way to do that is keep your head down and scurry home after dark. It's also embodied in a favorite saying in Bogotá: No dar papaya, or "Don't give the papaya," which means don't make yourself a target. But it's really a way for Bogota'nos to say that if you got robbed, it's your own damn fault for walking in the street, being gringo, flashing cash, whatever. Essentially, it's surrender to the criminal elements of Bogota', and it's because people are afraid to try to change things. With this in mind, remember Colombians, in general, are really friendly and warm, but making real friends in Bogotá is almost impossible.

"There are some key things to remember:

"1) Family is most important in the Latin culture, and especially so in Colombia. Friends are always secondary to family, and most people are taught from a young age that the only people you can really rely on are family. Most Bogota'nos spend their weekends hanging out with their relatives, rather than going out with friends.

"2) Colombia is a mountain culture, and mountain people tend to be really suspicious of new people. I've seen it with the Kurds in Iraq and Pashtuns in Pakistan. If you're in, you're like family and they'll literally take a bullet for you. But if you're not accepted, good luck. And it takes a lot of time and trust-building to be accepted.

"3) Bogota'nos work like donkeys. This city keeps farmers' hours, with lots of time at work. Late hours, high crime and bad traffic all conspire to keep people from going out with friends very much."

Betty paused to let that sink in for Buck and Rachael, then continued, "Only in Colombia have I really seen just how difficult it is to be poor in a relatively rich society. Poor people here are feared and almost despised by the middle class and upper class of the country. The city is evenly divided into geographical strata that determine the level of services and police protection an area receives. Poor areas get cheaper utilities, subsidized by the richer areas (thankfully!), but the cops won't go there, the (cheap) water is dirty, internet access is slow and unreliable and taxis are reluctant to enter."

As Betty continued to paint a dark picture, she said, "With that in mind, the people we have down there are secretive about their support of the U.S. or being against the drug cartels for fear of death. Our sources we have down there are not your typical Colombians; they will be some of the people from old Europe who have settled there and are considered to be rich. They have friends and connections outside of Columbia. You will need to find these people in different ways; i.e., you cannot approach them directly on the street or knock on their door in the middle of the day. Being seen with someone from America will be the last thing they want to have happen to themselves."

"So how do we approach them then?" Buck asked.

Betty looked at both of them and said, smiling, "I thought you would never ask. If there is a party or dinner with lots of people or if they're at the theatre, you should be able to make contact that way. Any other way they will pretend they don't know you and will walk away."

At this point she handed out pictures of people. Each picture was marked "Classified, For Official Use Only." Betty continued, "We have a few contacts down there and most of them are reliable and honest. The first one is Ernesto Johan Smith. He is a banker at the National Bank in the center of old Bogota'. If you're in trouble there, go to the bank and he'll be expecting you. The second photo you have there is of Ms. Carmen Youngblood. She is considered to be a socialite living on her dad's money, and she can be found with her escort of security people at the bars and clubs nightly in the new areas of Bogota'. As you can see, she is considered a beautiful woman and because of that she will not be hard to find in a crowd. The way to approach these two is with a password using the phrase of 'I love you' and 'I want to marry you.' They will answer back to you, 'Go away, you bother me.'"

With that, Buck and Rachael chuckled a little.

Betty smiled as well saying, "Just make sure that you and Rachael know which of you should say it properly and to whom."

"I'll take Carmen; you get the rich banker," Rachael said, looking at Buck.

"I was hoping I'd get the chance to try it on Carmen."

"I know; that's why you get the banker."

"It's probably better that way for you, Buck; at least, it may be safer," Linda said as she walked in.

"Damn skippy safer," Rachael added.

"How were your students?" Linda asked Betty.

"Just fine; I think they're ready for the big city of Bogota'."

"Thank you for your help, we have to do lunch one of these days if I can get away from work long enough," Linda said.

Betty smiled and said as she was leaving the room, "It's a deal."

Linda waited for Betty to leave the room before making eye contact with Buck and Rachael. She said, "There is someone I want both of you to meet, but it will be at the obstacle course at Homestead Air Reserve Base. We will break for lunch and go there this afternoon if that works for you two?"

"That would be fine; where do we meet for this?"

"We'll meet here and Evans and I will take you to the base and introduce you to the team you'll be working with. Let's say around 1:30 this afternoon."

With that, Linda was gone and Rachael looked at Buck. "Where to for lunch?"

Buck thought a moment. "How about the hamburger place down the street?"

"Sounds good."

At 1:30 both Buck and Rachael were standing in the foyer of the federal building when Evans and Linda came walking in from the parking lot. Evans looked at both of them. "Are you ready to go?"

Both Buck and Rachael nodded their heads in the affirmative and, with that, got into Evans' car and left for the Air Force Reserve Base. On the way there Evans told them, "The FBI headquarters wanted to say thank you for all that you two have done to assist us here. And I would like to thank you personally for everything you have accomplished thus far."

Linda turned and looked at both of them, "You don't realize the impact you have made being here--the leaks, Honduras, and what you're about to do."

"Aw shucks, we're here on vacation to see the big city," Buck replied. Then he added, "We couldn't stand by and let this happen to good people like you."

Evans and Linda sat there for a moment and Linda answered, "You don't know how much that means to us." She quickly turned away as she wiped a tear from her eyes.

When they reached the front gate to the base, Evans showed the guard his badge and said he would vouch for the occupants in the car with him. The guard saluted, "You may proceed."

With that, they made their way towards the base gym, where the obstacle course was. Once finding the gym, they parked their car and made their way to the obstacle course. From a distance, you could see some men running the course and others watching them workout. The closer they got to the men watching the others workout, they could tell that one of the men, who was holding a clipboard, was a captain and the other with a stopwatch was the master sergeant (MSgt.), who was doing all of the yelling at the men that were running.

"This is going to be fun," Buck said to Rachael.

"Shush, they might hear you," Rachael answered.

Evans and Linda were the first to introduce themselves to the captain and the

MSgt. At this point the captain told the sergeant to call the men in.

As they gathered around, the captain said, "I have some people to introduce to you; they're Special Agents from the FBI. These people are the brains behind our next mission into Colombia. You will treat them as one of the team, you will look out for them, they will look out for you; and if you do your jobs right, they will not need to be looking out for you, capiche?"

The team answered back with, "hoo-ah!"

"These two here (pointing at Buck and Rachael) found all by themselves a greenhouse full of poppy flowers and some marijuana plants and saved two hostages singlehandedly. So, don't think they are going to be dead weight on our mission. Yes, they're going with us and they're going to help us find a family being held by the cartel."

By now Buck and Rachael were turning red with embarrassment, although they tried not to show it.

"These other two agents are here to let you know that if we fail in our mission they will proceed to kick our butts for a proverbial long time so that we will have nothing to sit on. DO I MAKE MYSELF CLEAR?"

Another "Hoo-ah!" was heard from the team.

"Anything you want to add?" The captain looked at Evans and Linda.

Evans stepped up to where the captain was standing and said, "Gentlemen, this mission is a lot more than about finding drugs and rescuing people; it's about telling the bad guys who's really in charge. It's us, not them. We make the difference, we are the edge of the knife, we are the ones that will do the job and no one will know about it, except us. You know why? Because when you're the best, you don't need to brag; let your work speak for you. And the dead ones will speak volumes."

With that, the team all yelled, "Hoo-ah!" one more time.

"Is your team ready?" Evans said, looking at the captain.

The captain looked at the sergeant and he nodded, and the captain looked at Evans and said, "Ready when you are."

With that, the sergeant started yelling at the men to get back on the obstacle course. The captain walked with Evans, asking, "When do we leave, Sir?"

"We're ready when you are," Buck and Rachael replied.

"Take off is at 0500 tomorrow morning at the tarmac," Evans said.

"We'll be waiting," the captain said, and he turned around and headed back to his team.

"You'll be in good hands; I personally know the captain from other missions. I'd stake my life on him and his team anytime and anyplace," Evans said as he looked at Buck and Rachael.

Linda, standing a ways off, looked at them all. "Don't forget about the other part of the mission."

"I know I've asked you to do so many things of late, but I think you might like to be in on this. With all that has occurred with the leaks and all of our Intel blown, we need to put a dent in the cartel's network," Evans said as he looked at Buck and Rachael.

"What is it?" Buck and Rachael asked.

"We want to go after the kingpin. It would be a coup if we could catch him and bring him back to the states to stand trial for all of the damage he has done. He has embarrassed us and used our own people against us to get away with murder; we figure he has done enough," said Evans.

Linda at this point was watching and waiting for Buck and Rachael to answer.

"Oh sure, work for the FBI and see the world; I thought you'd never ask," Buck said as he looked at both Linda and Evans.

They all laughed and headed back to the car. After passing through the gate Rachael said, "Just like the old days, but now we get to go after the kingpin."

The rest of the day for Buck and Rachael was about getting their new equipment and stuff ready for the trip to Colombia. They were issued handguns with extra clips, compasses, sat phone and maps for Bogota' and the surrounding area.

As they packed their clothes into the suitcases, Rachael looked at Buck. "I want you to know that I couldn't have done any of the things we did before without you. You are my rock and my strength to carry on."

Buck came over from the other side of the bed and hugged her, "I couldn't have done any of this without you, either."

They kissed and stood there for a couple of minutes, both knowing they were about to do the impossible. They kissed each other again and Buck said, "I wonder if the old banker kisses any better?"

"For your sake, I hope he doesn't." Rachael laughed.

Both kissed again and said, "I love you" together.

CHAPTER IX

At 4:30 am Evans and Linda picked up Buck and Rachael from the hotel. Buck had already checked the two of them out of the hotel and turned in the car, and as the environmentalist would say, "They were clean and green to go." Evans opened the trunk of the car and helped Buck load their stuff into the trunk. Once done loading the trunk, both Buck and Evans got into the car, where Linda and Rachael were already seated and waiting. Linda handed them a box of donuts she had bought for both of them.

"It isn't much but I figured you wouldn't have time for breakfast this early in the morning, so I picked these up just in case you guys get hungry; and here is some coffee to wash down the donuts," Linda said.

"Thank you; only the best for the best," Buck said.

Nobody said anything the rest of the trip to the reserve base, each lost in their own thoughts and wondering how all of this would turn out. Rachael thought that when this was done they could go home. Buck was thinking that he missed his old stomping grounds and being a deputy and his friends back home. Linda was thinking that if they pull this off it would exonerate the mess and embarrassment the FBI had over all of this. Evans was deep in thought as well, wondering if it was right to ask his friends for so much. Nobody said a word, with everybody knowing what was at stake. It must work, it had to work; too many people were counting on it to work.

When they got to the front gate of the base, the gate guard checked Evans' pass and let them through. Driving to the far end of the base where the flight line was, you could see F-16s parked in a row. With their security lights on they looked benign. Sitting there they looked like big toys just waiting for a big kid to start playing with them. Evans parked in front of a building which had a strobe light on top, searching the sky for nothing and everything. The front of the building said, "Flight Ops Center" with the shield of the squadron right above it. The two big glass doors below the sign were open to allow the breeze to blow through. At this point Evans opened the trunk so that Buck and Rachael could unload their extra gear and suitcases. Evans had gone inside to check on the team and verify the trip was a go. He came back out and helped Buck and Rachael with their suitcases and took one of the bags himself inside to the flight ops, where there was a load master waiting to take their gear aboard the C-130 aircraft.

The team was already there waiting to board the aircraft as well. By now the captain was talking to Evans and the weatherman about the flight plan at the front desk. When both the captain and Evans were satisfied about everything for the flight, the captain told the sergeant to get them loaded onto the plane.

Evans came to where Buck and Rachael were standing. "Everything is good to go. I know I haven't said anything before, but I'll say it now." After a brief pause he grabbed Buck and hugged him and then Rachael, saying, "Thank you for all that you have done and Godspeed on your journey."

Linda was standing there with tears in her eyes, too emotional to speak. She hugged Buck and Rachael, saying through the tears, "Be safe and hurry home."

"As soon as we can," Rachael said as she stood there with tears streaming down her face.

"We'll be fine," Buck said as he looked the situation over, "and you owe us a dinner, which we are planning on collecting when we get back--deal?"

"Fair enough; it will be at our house-- deal?" Evans laughed.

"Deal," Buck said as he looked at both of them.

With that, both Buck and Rachael turned to see the C-130 cargo plane start its engines and come alive like a beast in the dark with red lights blinking and the ramp down in the back, loading the gear of the team and Buck and Rachael's things. After everything was loaded, the load master was outside the aircraft with headphones on, talking to the pilot and the crew chief inside the airplane. At a given command the airplane started backing up and turning around looking for the access to the runway to begin the final checks for takeoff. The pilot and co-pilot were busy inside doing their own part of the preflight checks, moving the tail stabilizer and wing controls, looking for anything out of the norm that might cause in-flight problems.

Satisfied, the pilot said, "Time to go."

The load master made a final check on the cargo inside the flying beast, and the crew chief sat in his own chair, watching the pilot and copilot finish their checks. Giving the all-clear, the load master started to close the ramp and seal everybody inside for takeoff. The giant aircraft rambled down to the end of the runway and sat there for the final checks before takeoff. The pilot and copilot sat watching the instruments in front of them as they revved up each engine separately, looking for problems. Finding none, the pilot and copilot revved all four engines at the same time, again looking for any problem.

"Tower, Flight 406 ready for takeoff on runway 180," the pilot notified the tower.

"Roger, Flight 406, you are cleared for takeoff on runway 180 degrees, turn to heading 190 and departure frequency 330," the tower replied.

"Roger, cleared for takeoff departure frequency 330," the pilot said.

The plane, with all four engines running high, sat there a second and then started rolling down the runway, when the pilot and copilot released the foot breaks. By now the noise of the engines was deafening inside the airplane. Everybody had their ear protection on and just sat there in the cargo seats along the length of the aircraft. The soldiers had their eyes closed, trying to sleep, and Buck and Rachael were wide awake, being a little nervous at first, having never been on a C-130 aircraft before. As the C-130 started rolling down the runway, pretty soon the jostling of the aircraft stopped; and all at once they were airborne. The pilot climbed to their assigned angels 130 and headed 190 degrees at 350 miles per hour. Inside the aircraft it was cold and still loud from the working engines. Rachael and Buck got as comfortable as they could in the cargo seats and tried to sleep like the soldiers around them. The flight would take approximately six hours and would land at the El Dorado Luis Carlos Galan Sarmiento International Airport.

As Evans and Linda watched the plane taxi to the end of the runway, they stood there looking at the flying beast with its blinking red lights and waited for the plane to takeoff. Once it made its way down the runway and was airborne, there was nothing more they could do, so both of them headed back to their car. Both Linda and Evans prayed that all the team aboard the aircraft, and especially Buck and Rachael, would come home safely with their prize. Once they could no longer see the plane, they got into their car and headed back to the federal office with the intent of cleaning house and starting the second step of the mission.

Once inside Evans' office, Linda and Evans sat down on the couch at the far end of the room. They turned the TV on the news channel and turned the volume up loud so they could talk without being heard. Evans used a writing pad to get things started. He wrote, "We need to send a message via the secretary to let the cartel know we are looking for the kingpin in Honduras based on our Intel sources."

Linda nodded in agreement and wrote back, "We need to make sure that the IT guys have a virus that send a signal we can follow from anywhere in Bogota'."

Evans agreed as well, writing, "Not too soon so we don't alert the kingpin."

Linda again nodded in agreement.

"Shall we begin?" Evans said, looking at her.

"I thought you would never ask," Linda replied.

With that, they left his office and walked down to the IT section and talked to Ron Echles, the IT chief.

"Anything new to report on your virus?" Evans asked Ron.

"We found a way to load it onto an e-mail and send it without setting any alarms off on the receiving computer," Ron replied.

Ron showed how it worked and what would happen when it was opened by whomever.

"All e-mails have their own characteristics, something like a fingerprint that identifies the source and sender. With that in mind, we can send an e-mail to another computer and track the e-mail via the fingerprint to wherever it goes without losing the e-mail, at the same time identifying the next sender and receiver of the same e-mail on whatever computer they use. Being able to do that, the virus will alert whoever is following the e-mail anywhere in the world because the virus will be on each and every computer it comes in contact with and will send a signal back to its origin. The best part is we can sit here and watch what happens with the e-mail and nobody will ever know were watching."

"I need you to send an e-mail from my secretary's computer and track it from down here. Can you do that?"

"When do you want to do it?"

"Right now. This is the message I want you to send: 'Joint operation with Honduran Army searching for poppy farms in southeast section of mountains near San Pedro Sula. Will fly to Nicaragua, continue joint search with Nicaraguan Army, same mission. Will complete in 30 days from this posting. Please disseminate accordingly.'"

Ron took the message and fed it into the computer e-mail system and sent the message via the secretary's computer. When done, Ron looked up and smiled, saying, "It should take a couple of days to track it to the final computer."

Evans looked at Linda and smiled and then looked back at Ron, saying, "Not a word about what we're doing here, and please keep me posted as to what's going on. When you need to talk, call me and I'll come down and we'll go from there, understand?"

"My place, your time," Ron said as he nodded his head.

"Step three next; are you ready?" Evans whispered as he and Linda left.

Linda nodded as they walked back to his office. When they both got to Evans office, they closed the door behind them. With that, step three began.

"You could get into a lot of trouble by doing what you're doing," Linda said, acting upset.

"Who you going to tell--my boss?" Evans replied.

"I would if it would do any good."

"Well, no one cares about the bad guys, especially if they can't find the bodies."

"It's against the law to kill just because they deal in drugs, and you know it."

"So what! We send one team down there to the kingpin's house, we take out his family and anybody else along the way; maybe he'll get the message not to sell drugs in the U.S. Besides, who cares if his friends and family die? Look what the leader in the Philippines has accomplished so far? We can set this up with the help of the military Special Forces, and they'll be in and be out before the bodies start to stink."

"What about the other cartels? What do you think they're going to do--stand there and let you do it?"

"That's the beauty of it; they'll be helping us take out the kingpin and they volunteered their soldiers to help us in this."

"So when does it start?"

"Started last week; we dropped them off in Panama and they should be there sometime next week. After watching my

116

daughter die from an overdose, all I can say is Karma is a bitch served cold."

"I hope nobody finds out about this; heads will roll over it if they do."

With that, Linda walked out of his office, slamming the door behind her. Evans sat at his desk and waited five minutes. When the phone rang, he picked it up and answered it. After a minute of listening Evans said, "I can't believe I've got to come down and solve this myself."

Evans slammed the phone down and left his office leaving the door open. When Evans got down to the cafeteria, Linda was seated at a table waiting for him there. Evans walked over to the table and sat down.

"Well, what do you think?" Linda asked.

"I give it a day and the SigInt should be able to pick up the chatter for us."

"What do we do about Rasmussen, now that we know what he's doing?"

"I've put a tail on him and I've got a warrant to search his place when the family is gone. I hope he knows the money he has in the other account has been traced back to a company that launders the money for the cartel in Columbia. It will all be seized when the time is right."

With that, they both went to their own offices and proceeded to do the daily grind of their jobs.

With everything set in place it would just be a matter of time before the fireworks would start. Rachael and Buck had their mission to perform, and the team was set up to work with the Colombian army searching for the kingpin, instead of the poppy farms. By the time the kingpin got word about the U.S. taking out his family and knowing that the other cartels were part of it, he would be on the move. The army would be following the computer signal generated by the e-mail virus. Life is good if you're smart. Not knowing who to trust and not knowing when the team would be there to take out his family, he would be running and hiding from everyone with his family in tow. This would slow him down, and he would be most vulnerable then.

CHAPTER X

Buck and Rachael were excited to be able to get out of the belly of the C-130 aircraft. After six hours of sitting in the cargo seats and freezing inside the airplane, it felt good to feel the warmth of the sun again when they stepped out onto the tarmac. The captain and the sergeant were busy getting the men and their gear situated before going off with their Colombian counterparts. The captain walked over to where Buck and Rachael were standing and handed them two packages. "You might want hang onto these, you never know when they might come in handy."

Buck opened his package and found it to be about a thousand dollars' worth, in Colombian pesos. The other package was the coordinates of where to meet the team incase anything went wrong. Buck and Rachael thanked the captain and grabbed their suitcases and made their way to the main building.

"Good hunting," the captain yelled out to them.

He turned to find the sergeant and his men and meet his Colombian counterpart.

Buck and Rachael made their way to the flight operations building, lugging their suitcases. Both of them were slightly winded when they got to the building. Fortunately, there were kids offering to help them as guides, willing to show off their city; such as, where to eat and what to see and do while there in the city. Buck and Rachael were overwhelmed at first but found a young man and asked, "What's your name?"

"Miguel."

The other boys, seeing that Miguel was picked to help, walked away downhearted.

"We need a hotel; can you help us find one?"

Miguel's eyes lit up and he started talking really fast, "I know a very good hotel, very few bugs. I will take you there. My cousin owns it, very clean."

Once they found a taxi they were off to the hotel. Miguel was showing off the city features as they rode in the taxi. Upon reaching the hotel Miguel did all of the talking to his cousin, making sure the room was clean and with a window pointing to the city. Once done, he helped cart the suitcases up to the second-floor room, talking about his cousin and, liking Americans, started asking questions about America.

"Someday I go there to school, get smart and come back here to help my family."

After getting to their room Buck handed him a hundred pesos. "We need to rest for about an hour; can you come back after that to show us the city?"

Miguel's eyes got big when he saw the pesos. "Yes, you will be ready in one hour; I will be waiting for you downstairs."

And with that, he was gone. Rachael smiled at Buck as the boy left.

"I think you made his day with the money."

"I hope so." Buck laughed.

Buck pulled out a map with the coordinates marked as to where the secretary's parents might be in Bogota'.

"Bogota' is twenty miles that way. How do you suppose we get there from here?" Rachael asked as she studied the map with Buck.

"Maybe Miguel will have an idea that might help us."

When the captain got back to his men, he asked the sergeant to do a quick function checkout on the electronic equipment they had brought with them. The sergeant called to one of the men to do an operations check on the electronic equipment. The soldier unpacked the equipment and did a check on it to see if it was working. After about five minutes he told the sergeant it was five by five and proceeded to pack it up again for traveling. The sergeant relayed the message to the captain and began to get his men squared away to board a two-and-a-half-ton truck that had been parked, waiting for them.

The captain's Colombian counterpart introduced himself to the captain and the sergeant. "My name is Colonel Montalba and I will be your eyes and ears on your mission."

"My name is Captain Tony Rich and this is Sergeant Michael Pena, we are pleased to be in your country to assist you in finding drugs."

"We will do good together finding the poppy farms and then we burn them," the colonel said, looking at the two men and shaking their hands.

After the men were loaded onto the truck, the colonel told the driver to take them to a certain place at the army camp, where the men would be housed until they left the next day. The colonel had his own jeep in which the captain and the sergeant rode as they followed the truck.

Rachael had finished checking out their electronic equipment for the third time.

"Are you nervous?" Buck asked as he was watching her.

"Should I be nervous?"

"Are you ready to go home?" Buck laughed at the question.

"I will be when this is done and we get back aboard the airplane."

"Seems like it has been years since we left Phoenix, and I never realized how homesick I could get being here. I miss the desert and our own jobs."

Rachael nodded in agreement and proceeded to check her weapon to be sure it was working fine. When they found everything in order, they stepped out of the room and headed downstairs to the front desk. Miguel was sitting there and got up when Buck and Rachael came down the stairs.

"Where would you like to go? Maybe eat or maybe see the town?" Miguel asked as he ran over to them.

"Are you hungry? I could go for some food myself," Buck said as he looked at Rachael.

"It's been a long day and I forgot about eating anything."

"I know a very good place to eat. My cousin has good food and will feed you well. Come follow me to my cousin's place," Miguel said.

"Miguel, how many cousins you got?" Buck asked as he smiled and looked at Rachael.

"Many cousins you all like," Miguel said as he turned and looked at Buck.

And off they went to find the cousin's place to eat.

"Miguel, do you have a cousin who has a car we can rent?" Buck asked after they had finished their meal.

"Si, I do have a cousin with a car to rent. Not far from here--you follow." Miguel laughed.

As they started walking to the cousin's place to get a car, Buck was looking around the area they were walking in.

"Miguel, are there any places we shouldn't go to?"

"Over that direction do not go, hate Americans, want money, and kill you for it."

"Good to know where not to be," Rachael said, looking at Miguel.

"We are here at my cousin's place," Miguel said after a few minutes.

"Where is the car?" Buck asked as he was looking the place over.

"Come, you see," Miguel said.

Miguel pushed the door open, looking for his cousin. When he found him, he spoke in Spanish, telling the cousin that the gringos wanted to rent a car.

"You want to rent a car?" He smiled and came over.

Buck nodded at the cousin. The cousin took them deeper into the back area of a garage and turned on the light. There, sitting in the dark, were three cars: a Mercedes Benz, Ford Explorer, and a '56 Chevy pickup, all in immaculate condition and pristine. You could tell the cousin had taken a lot of pride in these vehicles.

"Which one you want to use?" asked the cousin.

Buck's jaw dropped when he saw the vehicles, and all he could do was stammer a little. Rachael was just as surprised by what she saw.

"Can we borrow the Ford Explorer?" Buck said after finally after gaining his composure.

"Of course, you can," The cousin said.

"How much deposit do you want?" asked Rachael.

"How much you got?" The cousin asked, smiling.

"Not much, how about 10 thousand pesos for the week?"

Buck pulled out 10 thousand pesos and handed it to the cousin, who smiled broadly when he got the money and started yelling at the other family members to go get the keys to the Ford.

When the keys arrived, the cousin handed them to Rachael. "You better driver than man; you take the keys."

All Rachael could do was smile and giggle. Buck was amused and flabbergasted by this and laughed out loud. "If you only knew."

"You want to walk or are you going to let me drive?" Rachael asked as she smacked Buck in the shoulder.

"Now I can't drive; you gotta do it," Buck said, looking hurt from the slap as he grabbed his shoulder.

With that, they climbed into the Ford and drove out of the garage in the back of the house. With Miguel in the back seat they headed back to the hotel, parked out front and had Miguel stand guard by the Ford. A few minutes later Buck and Rachael loaded up the back with their gear, shut the hatch and climbed into front of the Explorer.

"We need to go to Bogota'. What is the fastest way to get there?" Rachael asked, looking at Miguel.

"I will show you easy way to Bogota'," Miguel said.

"We need to go to the bad area in Bogota' to find someone; are you sure you want to show us the way?" Buck asked.

Miguel stopped and thought for a moment, "You rescue people, yes?"

"Yes," Rachael replied.

"Then I will go with you," said Miguel.

Buck pulled out the map to show Miguel where they needed to go.

"I know this area--very dangerous, very bad people there. But I will show you," Miguel said.

When Rachael was on the outskirts of Bogota', she used the sat phone to call Evans back in Miami.

"Hello, I see you're on your way," Evans said when he picked up the phone.

"I'm calling for an update and to see if there were any changes to report before we go in," Rachael said.

"Hang on for a minute," Evans replied.

The line went silent and about 30 seconds later Evans was back on. "No changes to report from here. The address is located in the Villa Dos los Alles section of town. For the actual address you will need to use the electronic finder to locate the house they're in."

"Roger that and wish us luck," Rachael said.

"Good hunting and, remember, nobody is to know you were there," Evans replied.

Rachael closed the phone and put the Ford into drive and headed into the southern side of Bogota'. While driving into the city Buck pulled out his semi-auto pistol and checked to make sure there were two extra clips and put those in his pocket. He took Rachael's semi-auto pistol and made sure it was locked and loaded as well and handed her the extra clips for her to carry in her waistband. Miguel was watching all of this with big eyes, not knowing what to say. By now Buck had the electronic detector turned on and was giving directions to Rachael so that they could find the house. Miguel was telling Rachael the best streets to take as they followed the signal to the house. After about 30 minutes Buck told Rachael to stop the Ford.

"What do you think of that house there?" Buck asked as he looked out his window.

Rachael looked around until she saw the two men with the AK-47s standing outside the front of the house.

"I'm just guessing, but I think that's the house we're looking for," She remarked.

"How do you plan to do this?" Miguel asked as he was looking at the situation.

"I'm not sure yet," Buck said.

Rachael got out of the truck and walked around the vehicle to keep herself out of sight from the front of the house. Buck followed her moves just behind her.

"Is there another way into the house other than the front door?" Rachael asked Miguel.

"Si, there is a back door, I'm sure."

"How do you want to handle this?" Buck asked Rachael.

"I'm sure they have guards in the back of the house as well. The question is where are they? I think we would have better luck going through the back door instead of the front. It would be less obvious to all concerned," Rachael said.

"I have an idea. Take the truck behind the house and follow me," Miguel said.

With that, Rachael and Buck got back into the Ford and drove around to the back of the house. Rachael parked the vehicle a couple of blocks up so as not to attract any attention. All three walked down the back street to where they could see the house. As they stood there looking at the house, they could see two more guards standing outside on the porch in the shade.

"Wait for me to bring them to you," Miguel said.

Buck and Rachael looked at each other and nodded to Miguel and followed him to the house, hiding in the shadows of the surrounding houscs. From there Miguel walked over to the back of the house and picked up a rock and threw the rock at the bedroom window, breaking the glass. This got the guards' attention. They came out from under the porch awning and started cussing at Miguel for throwing the rock. At this point Miguel picked up another rock and threw it at the house again. One of the guards started running after Miguel and chased him to where Buck was waiting. When Miguel came running around the house where Buck was, he stopped and waited for the guard to come around. When the guard showed himself, Buck cold-cocked him as he cleared the house. Buck tied his hands behind his back and gagged him. They sat the guard up against the side of the house and out of sight.

"Do it again," Buck said to Miguel.

Miguel went back to the house with Buck dressed in the guard's clothes, pushing Miguel up to the porch of the house. The guard was smiling, thinking that his partner had caught Miguel, and wasn't paying attention to Buck, allowing him to walk up and butt-stroke the guard with his gun. Miguel and Buck quickly tied up the guard as Rachael came and watched for movement inside the house. Buck took the guard over to where the other one was being held.

"Bring the Ford to the back of the house and wait for us; we will be out shortly," Buck told Miguel.

Buck and Rachael entered the house and searched every room. As they cleared each room on the main floor, they then headed down to the basement. From the top of the stairs they could hear a TV. When Rachael crept down the stairs, she could see two old people sitting on the couch with a guard sitting close by, watching them. The two old people saw Rachael coming down the stairs. Rachael signaled with her finger to her mouth to be quiet. The volume of the TV covered up her descent down the stairs, and as she made her way to the guard, she hit him in the head with her gun. The guard never knew what hit him, and as she tied up the guard, both of the old people were amazed and just sat there. Rachael looked at them and pulled out a picture of Evans' secretary, and they began to talk all at once. Rachael motioned them to follow her up the stairs into the backyard.

Buck was watching the front of the house from inside the house, and the two guards in front were still standing there as if nothing was wrong. Rachael led the old couple out to the backyard, where Miguel was waiting for them. Miguel started talking to them in Spanish, telling them to get inside the truck and lie down. Miguel went with Rachael to gather the guards who were outside and put them downstairs with the other guard. Rachael then went into the house and started looking around, trying to locate the computer and anything else of possible value to the FBI and the other alphabets. Once she was clear, she gave the signal for Buck to leave.

As Rachael was looking around, Buck followed her and, looking into the kitchen area, found that the house stove was gas. He turned on the gas and cracked the light bulb in the kitchen and walked away. Getting into the Ford, they drove off as if they had been visiting someone. Within about two minutes they could see smoke coming from the direction they had just left.

"Oops," Buck said.

And nothing more was said.

Rachael drove the Ford out of Bogota' and back to the hotel where they were staying. The issue now was what to do with the old couple they rescued.

"Ask what they want us to do for them, now that they are free to go," Buck said to Miguel.

Miguel asked them and waited for their reply. The secretary's father said something and her mother agreed, raising her voice to show her support.

"They say they would like to go back home and be with their family," Miguel said after he had finished talking to them.

"Do you realize the bad people could come back to get you?" Buck said to the couple.

Miguel told them what Buck had said, and their reply was very humble.

"They say they have no other place to go and nobody to care for them," Miguel said to Buck.

Buck turned around and looked at the old couple and shook his head in agreement. With that, they drove to the hotel and stayed there the rest of the day. At this point Buck had Miguel, with the help of his cousin, arrange a ride for the old couple back to their home.

"The operation went well and the parents of the secretary are safe and sound," Rachael said to Evans when she contacted him on the sat phone.

"That's good news and I'm glad everything turned out okay," Evans replied.

"Isn't there a way that we can help these old people somehow?" Rachael asked Buck after she hung up the phone.

Buck thought a moment, "I just don't know what we can do for them. I feel the same way as you do. In the meantime, they can stay at the hotel with us while we wait for the team to show."

"I just feel bad for them, that's all. In the meantime, I'm going to play with the computer hard drive to see if there is anything of value that might help us in finding the kingpin," Rachael replied.

With that, Buck sat down on the bed and started going through the papers they found at the safe house. After a while Buck lay down, closed his eyes and was fast asleep. Two hours later Miguel came to their room and opened the door quietly and motioned for Rachael to follow him.

"I'm going downstairs to see what Miguel has to show me."

Buck was wide awake now and was ready to go down with Rachael as well. After securing the computer and the paperwork in a safe place, they headed downstairs. Miguel was already halfway down when he motioned to them to be quiet and then pointed to the door. There was his cousin standing at the door, talking to someone in the dark. When that someone left, the cousin turned and talked to Miguel very excitedly. Buck and Rachael waited to hear from Miguel.

"Some of the bad guys found out that two Americans were here at the hotel and wanted to know what they were doing here," Miguel said.

The cousin continued in Spanish, speaking to Miguel.

"We need to hide you from these bad men. They think you had something to do with the house catching fire in Bogota'," Miguel said after his cousin finished.

"How did they find out it might be us?" Buck asked.

"Nobody else would have done what you did, and they recognized my cousin's Ford," Miguel replied.

"What do we do now?" Buck asked Rachael.

"We could run and hide or run the risk of being captured by them," Rachael said as she shook her head.

"I know a place where you can hide and be safe," Miguel said.

"Where is that?" Buck asked Miguel.

"I will show you. The men looking for you are on the other side of town by now and we can escape in the darkness. But we must leave now."

As Buck and Rachael gathered their belongings, they made sure the computer and papers they found were with them, neatly packed away with their gear. Their suitcases would be extra weight and would hinder their leaving the town. With nothing but the essentials, they headed out into the darkness with Miguel leading the way.

CHAPTER XI

Buck, Rachael, and Miguel got to the edge of town and started making their way towards the mountains and the jungle. They looked at each other as they stopped to catch their breath, and Buck saw the look of determination in Rachael's eyes.

"Hell of a way to lose the belly fat," Buck said.

"Thanks for trying." Rachael laughed.

"We must hurry, and be quiet," Miguel said.

They both nodded and let Miguel lead the way out in their escape from town. After a number of minutes Miguel said, "Here is the trail we must follow to go into the mountains. Be very careful; the trail is narrow and the cliffs are deep."

At first the trail was friendly and the going was easy, but pretty soon they could tell the trail was getting steeper and the air was getting cooler. After climbing into the jungle for about an hour, they stopped to catch their breath again. Buck turned to see the lights of the town below him, and as he stood there looking, he wondered if they would ever see the town again. As they rested, both looked at each other, realizing they were breathing deeper and trying to catch their breath.

"We must leave now, sunrise soon, easy to find," Miguel said.

Rachael readjusted her gear with Buck's help tightening it, and they started moving again. As they continued into the jungle, the sun was starting to show itself on the trail. In the dark, all you did was keep your eyes on the trail in front of you; with the sunrise, you could see the jungle and the mountains. Everything was covered in green, and the mountains were almost vertical in their ascent to the sky. The trail became the only flat piece of ground they had to walk on. It was literally cut into the mountain, probably more out of necessity, for the locals who needed to get to the other side for whatever reasons they had. By 9:00 am the only thing that you could tell was manmade was the trail itself. Everything that resembled anything human was gone by now, swallowed up in the vast green sea of foliage and mountains. As they walked, the sun would occasionally shine through the treetops, hitting the trail as if it were a marker leading the way. After stopping to rest, Miguel, who was the only one unfazed by the climb, went back down the trail. After what seemed an eternity, Miguel came running up to where they were resting.

"They follow."

"How many?" Buck asked.

"All I could see was three. Mountain too steep for lazy men."

"Almost too steep for me," Rachael said.

With that, she got back up and continued to follow the trail deeper into the jungle. Miguel was still leading the way and would go forward and come back to check on the two Americans every so often. Miguel was like a mountain goat in his own world here, never breaking a sweat as he went back and forth on the trail. Both Buck and Rachael were sweating now, not only from the hike but also from the humidity in the air.

Miguel looked at both of them sweating and breathing heavily and said, "Not much further now; we almost there."

By midday the sun was straight overhead and you could barely tell, looking through the jungle canopy above. The trail looked like a tunnel you would find in a coal mine, dark and foreboding. The sounds of jungle life were loud enough to cover the noises they created as they kept going deeper into the mountains. Buck kept checking his compass to see what direction they were headed in. He could tell they were headed east, but with the trail winding through the mountains, that was all he could tell.

Miguel headed back down the trail to see how close the men were that were following them. He came back in about 15 minutes, smiling. "They still back there, but only two of them now follow."

"Can we stop them now?" Buck asked.

"Up ahead is a place to do so," Miguel said.

Buck was thinking that if they could get rid of these two henchmen, the traveling would be easier for them. After another hour of hiking on the trail, Miguel looked at Buck. "This place good for trapping men."

Buck and Rachael looked around the spot in the trail and noticed it was a flat opening in the jungle where you had about 20 feet of clearance from one side of the trail to the other side. It was an ideal place for an ambush.

"Walk back down the trail and wait for the guys that are following us. Then show yourself to them but don't get caught. Let them think you are hurt and can barely walk. Lead them here and we'll be waiting for them. When you get here, keep going; we will catch up with you as soon as we can," Buck told Miguel.

Miguel nodded in agreement and went down the trail.

"I'll be on the other side of the trail; that way we'll catch them in a crossfire," Rachael said.

"You read my mind; am I that easy to read?" Buck asked.

"I was thinking the same thing, only earlier. I was just looking for the right place

138

to pull it off. And in answer to your question, all men are." Rachael laughed.

"I'm a man. I can change if I have to, I guess." Buck laughed.

With that, they set themselves up on both sides of the trail and waited for Miguel to show. When Miguel finally showed, he was limping as if he had hurt himself. You could hear the men talking as they followed Miguel up the trail. When they got to the clearing, they slowed down, seeing Miguel up ahead resting against a tree. The two men looked at each other, smiling, knowing they had Miguel right where they wanted him. They hurried their pace to catch him. Miguel got up as if to run and fell on the ground, crawling towards the jungle. The two men were so intent on catching Miguel they didn't realize what was happening. Two shots rang out and both men fell to the ground dead on the trail.

Buck went over to check the bodies to make sure they were dead. Rachael kept him covered until she felt it was safe to come out from her vantage point. Miguel came back down the trail, watching Buck and Rachael go through the dead men's clothing, searching for anything that would hclp them. Miguel grabbed their weapons and held onto them. Buck and Rachael moved the bodies off of the trail and threw them into the steep gorge.

"No more follow us," Miguel said, smiling at Buck and Rachael.

Miguel hung onto the weapons as if they were trophies he had won in a game. The rest of the trip was uneventful and a lot less unnerving. They finally made their way to where Miguel had stopped. "We are here."

"Where is here?" Buck asked, looking at Miguel.

Miguel pointed to a place over in the shadows. "There."

Miguel led them onto another trail that was barely discernible, from the looks of it. As they went further into the jungle following Miguel, the trail opened up into a normal path, and from it you could see a river running down below. The sun was able to be seen clearly and unobstructed. Buck and Rachael stopped to take in all that they were seeing. It was a beautiful valley laid out in front of them and was breathtaking. Buck had never seen anyplace so pristine in his life.

"I wish we had a camera," Rachael said.

"You like? Very pretty here," Miguel said, and kept motioning them to follow him.

This time the trail went down and, instead of climbing up the mountain, they started down the trail to what looked like the bottom of the valley. Going another two hours on the trail, they ended up in a tiny remote village in what looked like the middle of nowhere. Miguel led them to the village leader and explained to him about their predicament. The village leader intently listened as Miguel went on saying these Americanos saved a couple from the cartel men, and now the cartel men were after them. The village leader spoke to Miguel in Spanish, and when he was finished, Miguel told Buck and Rachael, "Village elder say you are welcome here to stay here in the village, but you must not go past jungle without one of the men in village with you. Jungle very bad for you, other men from the cartel in jungle here, traps and other things in jungle."

Buck and Rachael nodded their heads in agreement.

"You are safe here and they will feed you well," Miguel said.

"Thank you very much." Buck stuck out his hand and shook Miguel's hand.

"I will come and get you when it is safe for you to come back." Miguel smiled.

In a moment, he was gone back up the trail and was out of sight. Buck and Rachael followed him with their eyes until he was gone and then looked at each other, with Rachael saying, "Let's go house hunting. I want a three-bedroom, two-bath, split-level entrance--what do you think?"

"I was hoping for a single-level, ranch-style home on five acres of land, for horses and maybe a cow or two," Buck said.

As they followed one of the men through the village, he took them to a hut with smoke coming out of the center of the open roof and pointed to them to go in.

"How did they know this is what we wanted all along?" Rachael asked, looking at Buck.

They went inside and, looking around the interior, Buck said, "It's a fixer-upper, but it's a place to start."

They unloaded all of their gear and lay down in the hammocks hanging from the posts of the hut and went to sleep. Buck and Rachael stayed inside the hut until dark, waiting to go out and try the sat phone. Calling out on the sat phone proved to be a problem, being totally surrounded by mountains that wouldn't allow the signal to leave the valley they were in. The only thing they could figure was there must have been something in the rock that absorbed the signal from the phone.

Buck looked around. "The only way to contact anybody is to go back up the trail on top of the mountains."

Knowing that there were people looking for them, Buck decided to wait and try later. Rachael agreed with his thoughts. "We need to be patient and wait till the fire dies down."

CHAPTER XII

Captain Rich and MSgt Pena got out of the jeep after arriving at the Colombian army base. The sergeant went to check the men into the barracks, where they would be staying between missions. The captain went with Colonel Montalba to the officers' quarters.

"When you're settled, I would like to go over the operation we have in mind for your team while you are here," the colonel said.

"Give me about 30 minutes and I'll be ready to go over the plans you have," the captain replied.

"We'll meet in the Officers' Club, and there you can meet my other officers who will be assisting us on these operations. Adios till then," the colonel agreed.

"Adios till then."

The captain went over to where the sergeant and his men were to see if everything was good to go for them. He found the sergeant checking on the electronic equipment and making sure it was stowed properly with the rest of the gear. The captain looked over everything himself. When fully satisfied, he went to check his team for their needs. The sergeant followed him over to the men, saying, "I hope this isn't a boondoggle like the last time, Captain."

"Come on now, we had a good time climbing the mountains in Nicaragua trying not to be seen and finding nothing of any value to take back for our efforts. It was like a paid vacation to the Garden of Eden."

The sergeant looked at the captain, who was grinning. "Yes, Sir, I remember it well, although your definition of the Garden of Eden and a vacation is a hell of a lot different than mine, Sir."

With that, they checked on the men; and after everyone was situated, the captain called all the men together. "Men, you know the drill; it's SOS DD DP (Same Old Stuff, Different Day, Different Place)."

The men nodded their heads in agreement.

"We are visitors in a foreign country. I expect you guys to be on your best behavior while here. Do not embarrass the U.S. Army in any way, shape or form, or there will be hell to pay, agreed?" continued the captain.

"Hoo-ah!" shouted the men.

"The sergeant and I will be briefed this afternoon by the colonel, and the sergeant will then brief you accordingly. Until then the time is yours to do what you want."

"Dismissed!" yelled the sergeant and followed the captain out of the barracks.

They reached the Officers' Club at 30 minutes past the hour, as agreed upon with the colonel. When they walked into the building through the front doors, the interior was somewhat dark and cool. Looking around, the captain saw the colonel and headed in his direction. The colonel was standing over a large table, looking at some maps and talking to the other officers standing next to him, explaining his thoughts about the location of some of the poppy farms. As the captain and the sergeant arrived near the table, the colonel introduced them to the other Colombian officers, and as he introduced each one, they clicked their heels together and stuck out their hand.

After the introductions were completed the colonel said, "I was showing my men where the possible sites are for the poppy farms in reference to the topography of the mountains. The elevation of the mountains provides a better opportunity for the poppies to grow."

The captain listened as the colonel explained where they would be looking by helicopter first, then by foot once the farms were located. Upon finding the farms they would burn and blow up the farms to destroy the crops, arrest the individuals running the farms and put them in prison.

The captain looked at the colonel, "What happens when the farmers are put in prison?"

"They stay a long time in one of our prisons at the hospitality of our government," the captain replied and, seeing the colonel was smiling, smiled back.

The colonel continued with his briefing, telling everyone, "Tomorrow we'll be flying over these spots on the maps, and from there I will determine where we go on foot--any questions?"

None of the Colombian officers had any, and the colonel looked at the captain, who shook his head no.

"We will use two helicopters. My men will be in one helicopter; the captain's men will be in another. We will split up and the captain will go into this area and we will go into this other area," the colonel said, pointing at the map.

The colonel gave the captain a map of the area he was to explore, saying "Good hunting, Senor." The captain then gave the map to one of the junior officers for safekeeping, whereupon the colonel said, "We will be leaving in the morning around 6:00 am. Please be ready to go."

After the captain left with the sergeant, the colonel looked at his men. "We will fly over this area, and if we see anything, we will land and start a few fires on the junk piles and make sure we get pictures before and after to show our American friends we are serious about the drug problem here in Colombia."

The other officers laughed and smiled as they headed out the door of the Officers' Club.

The captain went back to his room and sat there, trying to collect his thoughts about the mission for tomorrow morning. He knew the sergeant would get the men ready by 6:00 tomorrow morning. This would be his third time out in the country, and each time he learned a little more about the people and their cultures. He also knew not to turn his back on the host military personnel. He had learned by the sad experience of losing two men that greed doesn't stop with the uniform. He had his own scar where a bullet creased his arm while trying to save the two men. He knew after he filed his report about the incident that it would be covered up by our own people in order to maintain good public relations with the country. Those responsible for killing the two men were summarily shot while in the field by the officer in charge--jungle justice for the drug war. Michael Pena had been with him on that mission and was instrumental in keeping the other team members alive; in fact, if it hadn't been for him, more would have died. He shot one of the national soldiers before he did any more damage. His men on the team knew their business and had learned to keep a wary eye on their confederates in arms. The men learned that in order to survive they were the only ones they could count on. Most of the men were seasoned and knew what to do; the rookies would have the sergeant riding their backsides to keep them safe. After thinking a little on the mission, he laid down on his bed and was fast asleep in seconds.

At 0500 am the captain was already awake, shaved and showered. Putting on his uniform, he had a bulletproof vest on under his top shirt, which would protect his vitals in case something went wrong in the field. All of his men had them. It became a requirement that he had initiated after his two men were killed--a lesson learned the hard way.

As he stepped out into the darkness, the sergeant came running up to him. "The men are ready to go, Sir."

"Thank you, Sergeant. Was everybody on their good manners last night?"

"Yes, Sir, they were all choirboys last night, Sir."

"That's good to hear, Sergeant."

When the captain arrived, the sergeant had the team fall in line. When they were all standing at attention, the sergeant put them at ease.

The captain waited until the men were at ease. "Men, I appreciate you minding your manners last night and want you to know that Colombia is a little safer with you here."

All the men laughed at this.

"You all know the drill here. I ask you to be professional in all that you do here and in the field today. Watch out for each other and don't take anything for granted. If you see something that does not look right, tell the sergeant and, if necessary, tell me. We will go from there to figure it out, understood?"

The men let out a "Hoo-ah" and were silent again. The captain looked at the sergeant. "Sergeant, you have your orders; proceed."

At this, the captain walked away a short distance and the sergeant took over, making sure the men were ready for the operation. Five minutes later a truck pulled up along with a jeep to transport the men and the captain to the airfield, where they would board the helicopters.

When they arrived at the airfield, the colonel was waiting for them with his men. The American team got out of the truck, and the sergeant got them in a single line in order to load the helicopters. The HH-60s were brand new to the Columbian army, and the pilots were freshly trained and back from the U.S.

The colonel walked up to the captain. "I trust you slept well last night, Captain?"

"Like a baby, Sir."

With that, the colonel pointed to the second helicopter, "This one is for your team."

"Permission to board, Sir?"

The colonel nodded his head yes and, with that, the captain told the sergeant, pointing at the second helicopter, "Get them aboard."

The sergeant took over the boarding of the helicopter and stowing their equipment. The colonel yelled in Spanish to one of his officers to load their men into the first helicopter. A smaller Huey helicopter was warming up as well. The captain looked at the colonel for a moment, and the colonel said, "I will need to have a separate helicopter for myself and the camera crew to take pictures of what we find." The captain nodded at this and took off to get aboard the helicopter.

Within five minutes all three helicopters were airborne and gaining altitude to clear the jungle surrounding the base. The colonel's helicopter went with the MH-60 side by side into the mountains to the east of the base. The captain and his crew went to the west of the base into the high country.

The Sikorsky MH-60 helicopters took the place of the HH-3E Jolly Green Giant helicopters as the new Pave low for the U.S. Air Force and the U.S. Army. The MH-60G

Pave Hawk's primary mission is insertion and recovery of special operations personnel, whereas the HH-60 is used for recovery of personnel under stressful conditions, including search and rescue, emergency aero medical evacuation (MEDEVAC), disaster relief, international aid and counter-drug activities. The helicopter models the Colombian army was flying were the HH-60s version, minus some of the electronic equipment of their American counterparts.

The blast of cold air from the speed of the helicopters had everybody aboard freezing, and the higher they climbed the colder it got. They left the side door open for the purpose of searching for the poppy farms. Once reaching the mountain range, the pilots looked for a valley to climb through to get up the mountain. Both sides of the helicopter were now looking for the farms and staging areas for making the tar heroin.

After searching one ridge of mountains they would find another and follow that ridge line down into the canyon. On the second ridge one of the spotters saw a poppy field down below. The spotter handed his binoculars to the captain and pointed to the field. After the captain saw the field of poppies below he called the pilot of the helicopter through his headset. The pilot then turned around to catch a view of the field himself.

After a couple of more passes over the area the pilot put the helicopter into a hover about a quarter mile from the farm. The team went down the rope lines to get to the ground. Once on the ground, the team set up in a defensive configuration until all of the team was on the ground. Once the helicopter was away and the dust settled, the men made their way to the poppy field, moving in a single-file line. At the command of the sergeant, one of the men took the point and was ahead of the team by 30 yards, looking for booby traps and the bad guys.

As they moved closer to the farm, the men slowed down, looking in all directions. The point man raised his hand in a fist and motioned for the captain and the sergeant to come forward. The team went into a slouch position to cover themselves in the jungle. As the captain and the sergeant moved forward, they could hear voices coming from further up the trail. This time the sergeant got down on his belly and moved forward, crawling up the trail, the captain closely following. They both stopped at a small clearing along the trail and kept listening to the voices. The sergeant looked at the captain and motioned with his hands about going a little farther to get a better picture of the situation.

The captain, using his hands, said, "Be careful; don't get caught."

With that, the sergeant inched closer until finally he could see the men talking. Both had AK-47s slung on their backs. There were three of them smoking cigarettes and talking about last night's activities at the cantina. The sergeant made his way back to the captain and apprised him of what was ahead on the trail.

The captain thought for a moment and asked the sergeant, "Is there any other way around them to the farm?"

"No, not that I could see."

"Let's get the team up here and try to capture them; if not, we will need to silence them."

Quietly, the team moved into position through the jungle around the three men. Once the team was in place, the signal was given by clicking twice on the radio. The sergeant yelled to the men in Spanish, "Put your guns down, you're surrounded."

At first the lead man dropped his AK-47 into the firing position and fired a burst in the direction of the sergeant's voice. He was shot by one of the men covering him from the right side of the trail. The other two men, seeing their leader go down holding his shoulder, dropped their weapons to the ground and raised their hands into the air. Two of the team moved forward, forcing the two guards onto the ground, using plastic ties to bind their hands behind their backs. Pulling the two men to their feet, the captain went over to them and started asking questions about any booby traps and how many more men were guarding the field. The men refused to answer the captain's questions; therefore, the captain put one of them on point leading his men to the field. As they made their way to the field, the one man stopped and wouldn't go any further. The sergeant went to where the man was standing and looked around. In about two minutes he a found a small string across the trail they were on and cut the line. He followed each string to find the end of it attached to a claymore mine. The sergeant diffused the claymore and threw it away into the jungle.

From that point on the team moved swiftly, following the trail until they got to the farmer's field. The captain motioned one man to stand guard over the three Colombian men. The others of the team moved around the field, making sure not to be seen. As they made their way around the field, the captain could see some thatch-roofed buildings on the other side of the field. The captain assumed these buildings were for refining the opium into bricks.

The sergeant called on the radio, saying there were three more guards on the other end of the field. They were guarding the workers that were busy mixing the lime into the barrels of boiling water. The captain thought it must be harvest time. With that, the sergeant made his way to the captain. Once there, the team moved in, catching the three other guards unawares and the workers red-handed, so to speak, making the tar. After the area was secured they called for the helicopter pilot to land near the buildings.

At this point the colonel was notified about their finding the poppy farm. He replied he would be there in 20 minutes. At that point, the team proceeded to burn the fields and destroy the buildings, using satchel charges they had brought with them. In all, it took about 10 minutes to set the place on fire and destroy the buildings. When the colonel landed, he had his camera team out first, taking pictures of him leaving the helicopter then taking pictures of the field on fire and the buildings lying in heaps as they burned and smoked from the satchel charges. The colonel looked pleased with what he saw and asked where the workers were. The captain replied they're right over with the guards. The captain showed the way to where they were being held. The colonel motioned for his men to follow him to where the prisoners were, forming a line in front of the men being held.

As the colonel looked at the captain, he shook his hand. "Congratulations on finding the field and catching these men. You have done well."

The camera crew had followed the colonel to where the prisoners were, taking pictures of the colonel shaking hands with the captain as the colonel faced the camera, smiling. After the photo session was over, the camera crew left and boarded the helicopter they had come in, waiting for the colonel to follow.

The captain looked for the sergeant and asked him, "Any problems with the men?"

"No, Sir, not even a scratch or a torn fingernail."

"Good, get the men to the chopper. We still have some daylight left to go hunting for some more poppy fields."

About that time gunfire erupted and the captain, looking around, realized that all of the prisoners were dead. He looked at the colonel with a look of "What the hell are you doing?"

The colonel replied to the look, "Don't you think our rehab program works well?"

The captain was dumbfounded at the audacity of the colonel taking the prisoners' lives. But held his tongue and headed back to the helicopter with his men. After telling the sergeant about what had happened to the prisoners, he sat a moment and then told the sergeant, "Watch your back with this colonel and his men."

He nodded in agreement with the captain. "If anything goes down, he goes first."

The rest of the trip looking for the poppy farms was a bust; nothing else was found. They returned to the base and landed just in time to see the colonel's helicopter come in on final approach and land with the other HH-60 right behind him.

The colonel got out of the helicopter and walked over to the captain, smiling. "We found two more farms and destroyed both of them. No prisoners to speak of; they must have heard our helicopters flying and took off into the jungle."

The captain congratulated the colonel on his success. "I need to get back to my men and get them squared away for our mission tomorrow."

"Not a problem, we will go tomorrow same time, only this time we will go north and south. I will see you tomorrow, then?" The captain nodded in agreement and turned and walked away towards his men, who were unloading their equipment from the helicopter.

The captain, looking for the sergeant, asked, "Anybody seen the sergeant?"

"He made a beeline for the privy, Sir," one of the soldiers said.

The captain laughed at this and headed towards the closest building, looking for the sergeant. He found the sergeant as he was leaving the bathroom. "Did you get any signals from the electronic equipment today?"

"Only a faint one on the first ridge, then it disappeared. What are we looking for, Sir?"

The captain and the sergeant walked back outside the building. The captain, looking around to make sure they were alone, said, "The Intel weenies have found a way to track e-mails between the cartels and their people inside the cartels. If we can locate the signals, they may lead us to the kingpin. Our real mission here is to bring the kingpin back with us to stand trial in the U.S."

The sergeant stood there thinking, and a slow whistle came from his lips. "How are we supposed to do that, Sir?"

The captain explained the plan to him. "We have another team waiting for word to come in with an American helicopter and fly him out of here to Panama, where he will be transferred by plane by the FBI to Washington, D.C."

"Where is this other helicopter that's waiting for our word to fly?"

"The CIA has it."

"Good enough for me and way above my pay grade to worry about. So how do we get the helicopter pilot to take us back to where we got the signal?"

The captain smiled and said, "Sergeant, I have faith in you; you'll find away," as he continued walking.

The sergeant stopped in mid stride and looked at the captain. The sergeant didn't know whether to hit or thank him. The sergeant, grumbling under his breath said, "Yes, Sirrrr."

Starting to walk again, he was still grumbling after getting over the shock of the captain's request. He caught up with the captain in two steps and they made their way to the rest of the team on the flight line. They called for a truck, which came and picked them all up and took them to their barracks.

Later in the evening, as the captain was eating his meal, the sergeant knocked on his door. The captain opened the door and invited him in. "What brings you here into officer country?"

"I was thinking about how to get the helicopter pilots to fly back where we were today to see if we can pick up that signal again."

"What did you come up with?"

"Well, Captain, just short of commandeering the helicopter, maybe we could bribe the pilot and the copilot with money or something."

"What did you have in mind to bribe them with?"

"Well, Sir, the booze here is pretty expensive for the locals, most of which none can afford, even the officers in the Colombian military. I was thinking if you would buy the good stuff maybe that would work for them to fly us to where we needed to go."

"How much are we talking about, Sergeant?"

"Well. Captain, I was thinking a bottle of good whiskey for each one of them might work. It would only be 100 dollars for two bottles, and I know where we can get our hands on some good American whiskey."

The captain looked at the sergeant, not knowing what to say but realizing it was a good plan and asked, "How soon can you get it?"

"We'll need you to buy it, Sir, because being an officer and all, they won't question you about the whiskey, Sir."

The captain smiled at being caught in his own game. "Lead the way, Sergeant."

The captain and the sergeant made their way to the local bar on the base and found what would be considered a class 6 store, where they sold all kinds of liquor. The captain paid for the whiskey and, as they were coming out of the store, gave it to the sergeant. "You sure this is going to work?"

"I think it should, Sir; we'll find out for sure tomorrow when we take off."

The next morning the teams showed up with their gear on the flight line and were already loading their equipment onto the helicopters when the captain showed up. The colonel was busy getting his men onto their helicopter, along with the camera crew in the Huey helicopter. The sun was just starting to peek over the mountain when the teams were set to take off. The captain's helicopter waited for the colonel's helicopter to take off before leaving the flight line. After a minute of flying south the helicopters turned and headed west to where they had been yesterday. The captain looked at the sergeant, who was smiling as he gave a "thumbs up" signal. With that, the captain sat back and enjoyed the ride. In the meantime, the soldier carrying the electronic gear had his head phones on, listening for a signal. Within 30 minutes they were over the same ridge of mountains as yesterday, and the captain and the sergeant were watching the soldier with the head phones on. In about two minutes he picked up the signal again, showing a "thumbs up" sign. With that, the captain told the sergeant not to lose the signal and to direct the pilots to where they needed to go.

In about 10 minutes they were on top of the mountain, looking down into the valleys. One of the spotters caught sight of a small house and told the sergeant by tugging on the sleeve of his shirt and pointing in the direction of the house. The sergeant looked at the captain and pointed down. The captain grabbed the binoculars and took a look for himself. The captain saw people down below moving around, apparently not concerned about the helicopter overhead. With that, he got the coordinates of the house from his GPS. He told the radio operator for the team to contact Blackbird 1 on frequency 230.12 and tell them that it appears they've found what they're looking for at these coordinates. Once making contact, the radio operator sent the signal to Blackbird 1 and confirmed that the message was received. When this was completed, the captain asked the sergeant to have the pilots find a spot not too far away to land. The pilot nodded his head and proceeded to find a place they could exit the helicopter. The pilot took it back to the other side of the mountain so as not to alert the people in the house below, and finding a flat spot on top of the mountain, landed.

The captain looked at the soldier with the electronic gear, "Are you still getting the signal?"

"Yes, and it's stronger, Sir."

The captain looked at the sergeant. "You ready to go hunting, Sergeant?"

"Yes, Sir, three bags full, Sir. But we'll need to leave a couple of our people here to keep an eye on the helicopter; the whiskey will only go so far, Sir."

The captain agreed. "Pick two men who will make sure we have a ride back when it's time to go."

"Yes, Sir. Murphy and Smith, you two stay here and watch the helicopter; don't fly away without us."

The other team members loaded up their equipment and made ready to climb down the mountain. With the point man out about 50 yards, the team moved on down the mountain, slowly following the point man. The going would be easier knowing that there were no booby traps on the mountain. As they made their way, the captain checked with his radioman for any communication with Blackbird 1; finding none, they continued down the mountain. When they got closer to the house, the captain and the sergeant went a little closer to get a look at the setup of the house. The captain used his binoculars to see if there were any movements outside the house. At first the captain didn't see anything, then caught the smell and smoke of a cigarette near the front door. He watched for a moment and then he saw a man with a pistol and AK-47 over his shoulder. He motioned to the sergeant to come down to where he was lying. The sergeant crept over to the captain and lay down next to him. The captain gave his binoculars to the sergeant, and he took a look for himself. When the sergeant was finished looking, he handed them back to the captain. Then they made their way back to where the team was hiding.

Once they caught their breath, the captain looked at his men. "There's a VIP down there; can't tell who it is, but there is a guard at the front door watching the place."

The team members smiled when the captain told them the news. It had to be somebody important for a guard to be there as well. The captain looked at the sergeant. "What do you think will work to get us down there and back safely?"

The sergeant drew the layout of the house and surrounding area, pointing to two of the soldiers. "Two of you go around to the back of the house in case they try to escape out that way," and then pointing to two other soldiers, "You two sit in front and watch to make sure nobody else surprises us. The captain and I are going to take out the guard in front of the house."

"Be careful and be ready for any kind of surprise they might throw at us. Are you ready?" The captain asked.

The team nodded in the affirmative and separated into teams of two and made their way to their positions, awaiting the signal from either the captain or the sergeant. The captain and the sergeant waited for the team to be in place before they made their move on the guard. The captain waited five minutes and nodded at the sergeant for them to make their move. After crawling through the deep underbrush, they finally got in position to attack the guard. The sergeant was closest to the guard, but because the guard was standing at the front door it would require the sergeant to be in the open for too long. The captain, seeing the problem, decided to create a noise to draw the guard away from the house. He thought for a moment and made a turkey call from where he was in the brush. At first the guard didn't notice, so the captain did it again. This time, not knowing what the sound was, the guard left his position to check it out. Walking around in the front yard looking for where the sound came from, the captain did it again. The sergeant was able to get behind the guard and put a choke hold on him, dropping him to the ground. They dragged the guard into the jungle, where the two teams were waiting, then bound and gagged the guard to keep him quiet.

The captain then moved to where the guard had been standing near the front door. He waited for the sergeant to join him, and at the count of three they busted down the door to the house. After screaming at the occupants inside the house, the back door flew open and a man took off running into the jungle. One of the team went after the man and caught him quickly, as he was so out of shape. After searching each one of the rooms inside, the captain found a couple of young ladies inside one of the rooms, sleeping. They were brought out into the front room and then outside with the man. The sergeant came out of the house, holding the computer the man had. After lining up the ladies and the man, the captain told his men to search the man for some ID. Finding his wallet in his pants, the man was identified as Juan Diego Ortiz. The ladies gave the captain their names as Maria and Consuela and said they had been hired to keep the man happy until the men who had hired them would be back to pick him up. The captain asked the girls if they knew who the man was. One said he was a dirty old man; the other said he has something to do with cartel business.

"When are the other men coming to pick him up?" the sergeant asked.

"Not sure, maybe today," Maria answered.

The sergeant looked at the captain. "Do we take a chance and wait or do we take off?"

The captain thought about the question for a moment. "A bird in the hand is better than two in the bush; let's get back to the helicopter. Whoever this guy is, they have him hiding out in this house in the middle of nowhere for a reason. He must be pretty important or he would be dead by now. Let's move it."

With that, the sergeant gathered the team together and sent one soldier to be point for the trip back up the mountain. As they started back up into the jungle, the last soldier looked back and saw three trucks coming up to the house. He signaled for the sergeant to come back and take a look. The team stopped and crouched down in the shadows of the plants. The captain came back to see for himself what was going on. Upon seeing the three trucks, he took his binoculars and looked to see who it was. One of the vehicles was a Cadillac Escalade, and as he watched the Escalade, a family got out of the vehicle. The captain also saw a short man get out of the front of the first truck. You could tell he was in charge by the way he ordered the men around. The captain gave the binoculars to the sergeant. "Look at the small man giving the orders down there."

The sergeant studied the man for a minute, then moved the binoculars away, and then brought them back up for a second look at the man. He looked at the captain and smiled. "I think I recognize the small man down there."

The captain looked at the sergeant and both of them said at the same time, "KINGPIN." The captain called for the girls to come back. The sergeant told the girls to look down into the area where the house was. "Who is the small man down there?"

Consuela recognized him immediately. "He a very bad man and kills people for fun."

The captain looked at the sergeant as the sergeant said, "Are you thinking what I'm thinking?"

The captain nodded yes. "But what do we do with the rest of these people?" The captain, thinking further about this for a moment, continued, "This is too good to pass up and it might be our last opportunity to catch this guy."

"I agree with you on this, but the question remains, what do we do with these other people?"

"We have eight men to work with here and they have at least six guards down there to watch over shorty and family. I think we can take out the six guards by killing them, kidnap the family and hold them here in the house until Blackbird 1 comes. Then we can get him, family and all."

The sergeant looked at the captain. "We'll have to be real quiet to get away with it."

"Yes, we will."

And with that, the captain told the sergeant, "Tie those people to a tree and gag them to keep them quiet. Keep one man to guard them and tell the soldier if they make a run for it, kill them quietly. Sergeant, get the men ready to go back down there."

With seven of them going back, they made their way down to the house. Once in position, each man had a target to take out. Each team member had been chosen especially for this kind of mission, each trained in search-and-destroy tactics as the situation required. Each man was capable of doing what was required instinctively in the moment of need. As the team sat there watching the guards, they could see four guards outside the house patrolling the area. Each guard could see the others at any given time. The team had to strike all at the same time, or one of the guards would alert the other guards and the two inside. As each team member crawled up to their target, they waited until the other team members were in place, and at exactly the same time the men grabbed their targets, covering their mouths and sticking a knife into the base of their skull, twisting the handle of the knife inside and slowly letting the target fall silently to the ground. With the help of the other team members, they dragged the guards away into the jungle, covering them up with dirt and palm fronds. That left the two guards inside to be dealt with.

Silently reaching the house, the captain and the sergeant moved towards a window, looking inside to find the guards. Both were in the front room, playing cards to pass the time. The captain looked at the sergeant and whispered, "How do we get the guards out of the way?"

169

"How about we knock on the door and when one of the guards answers the door, we rush in, kill both guards at the same time."

"What about the kingpin; he may have a gun as well."

"Maybe we can use the guards as shields. We can knife the first guard at the door and then the second one as he gets up to see where the first guard went."

"How is your Spanish; is it enough to be an annoyance for them to come out?"

"I hope so."

The sergeant walked up to the door and knocked. A voice from inside asked, "What do you want?"

"I need to use the bathroom," The sergeant said.

"Use the jungle, you idiot!" The voice called out.

The sergeant knocked on the door again, "I need some toilet paper."

By now one of the guards, grumbling, got up to open the door; and as he opened the door, the captain grabbed him and stuck a knife into his chest, pulling him away from the door. The other guard got up to see what the noise was, and as he made his way to the door, the sergeant put his knife into the guard's throat, cutting his wind pipe and the main artery in his neck, therefore quickly bleeding him out. Two of the soldiers came running up to the house and joined the captain as they made their way inside. The captain and the others checked the other rooms to make sure they were clear before moving on to the one room where the family was. The captain told the men that were with him to go outside to the back of the house and break a window, and that would be their cue to come through the bedroom door. The soldiers went out to the back of the house and, when ready, broke the bedroom window. A second later the captain broke down the door, catching the family sleeping. The short man looked into the semi-auto the captain was carrying and raised his hands over his head and pleaded with the captain not to shoot his family. The captain thought this was ironic, simply because this man was responsible for the murder of so many thousands of people-- men, women and children--and here he is begging the captain not to shoot his family. If anybody deserved to die, this is the one who did the most.

By now the rest of the team showed up and tied the family up with paracord and plastic ties. The captain sent a runner up to where the radio was waiting and told him to send a message to Blackbird 1 to come and get the pigeon crap and to bring the other people down to the house. In about ten minutes the team was all together again. The ladies and kids were in the bedroom being watched by two soldiers; the kingpin and the old man were in the front room sitting on the couch, sweating like stuck pigs. The radio man had received a message that Blackbird 1 was in route for the pickup. In twenty minutes, they could hear a helicopter coming up the canyon, and the captain told the sergeant to pop smoke to let them know where they were.

The radio man got on the radio, "Do you see smoke?"

"Yes, the color of smoke is green," The pilot said.

"Affirmative, come on in."

When the helicopter landed, the team, realizing they were Americans, came out of the shadows and waited for the two civilians to get closer to meet them. The two civilians showed their IDs and said, "Let's see what you have."

Upon reaching the door the captain met the men. "Welcome to our house, gentlemen."

When the civilians saw the two men sitting on the couch, their jaws just about hit the floor. Both looked at each other, excited at what they were seeing before them. The first civilian said, "Do you know who you have here?"

"I know one of them is the kingpin; the other I don't know," the captain replied.

"The second man is the bookkeeper for the cartel. He knows where the money is coming from and who it's going to," said the second civilian.

With that, they loaded the old man and the kingpin and his family, along with the two ladies and the guard, into the helicopter and watched them take off into the sky.

"Well, Captain, we did good today," said the sergeant.

"Yes, Sir," the captain said, adding, "Maybe we can go home now."

Later that afternoon the team made it back to the helicopter and rejoined the other two soldiers. The captain asked the two who had stayed behind, "Any problems here on this end?"

"No sir, once we got their attention, not a problem at all," answered one of the men as he patted his rifle.

"I'm glad to hear that soldier," the captain said, grinning.

After looking at his watch, the captain realized he and his team had been down in the valley nearly all day, approximately eight hours. Thinking to himself six bad guys dead, no good guys hurt--not a bad day for the fish we caught. All the way back to the base the team sat there in the helicopter, saying nothing, acting as if nothing had happened, just another day fighting the drug war in a country that's more corrupt than the cartels.

When they landed at the base, the colonel was waiting for them. "How was your hunting today, Captain?"

"We found one place that had been used a while back, so we destroyed it to be sure it wouldn't be used again."

"Sorry to hear that. We had better luck; we found two poppy farms and destroyed them. Plenty of pictures taken today."

The captain looked at the colonel, who was smiling. "Congratulations Colonel, that is good news. We'll be leaving tomorrow as we've found just a few poppy farms here. I'll inform my superiors that you are capable of handling the poppy- farm eradication by yourselves. Now if you'll excuse me, Colonel, I need to make sure my men are squared away."

As the captain walked away, he thought to himself, "How many people did you rehab today?" And as the colonel stood there and watched the captain walk away, he thought to himself, "What fools these Americans are for trying to stop the drugs they would die so badly for." And both were right in their thoughts.

Chapter XIII

When Evans got the news about the capture of the kingpin and one of his money men, he was elated that the plan had worked. Now his main concern was with Buck and Rachael and where they were. He called Linda into his office to share the news about the kingpin. She was relieved to hear of the capture, as well. As she was concerned for both Evans and herself, she asked, "What about our two friends?"

"Haven't heard word yet. I think they're okay. As the old saying goes, no news is good news."

"I hope you're right."

At this point Evans got on the phone and called the security team. "Pick up Rasmussen and bring his ass to my office with an escort; also send the IT security team in and tell them to come get the bugs out of the building."

The next few days were going to be hectic for Evans and Linda. The fact they had the kingpin was a closely guarded secret for the time being. The kingpin and his bookkeeper were arraigned in federal court the same day they landed in Washington D.C. They were sent to the federal detention facility in solitary confinement, stripped down to their briefs in a bare cell with no bedding of any kind, so they couldn't commit suicide. The men would be interrogated by all of the alphabets shortly for what they knew about the drug trade in the U.S. The kingpin's family was sequestered under armed guard in an old farmhouse in the outskirts of Virginia. The wife of the kingpin was wondering what would happen to them. One thing for sure, this family wouldn't disappear like some of the families had in Colombia and old Mexico.

Buck looked at the stars in the night sky, wondering if they were the same stars they saw in Arizona. He looked around and noticed that Rachael was readying herself for the hike up the mountain to make the phone call back to civilization. One of the people from the village was waiting to take them to the top of the mountain and bring them back down again safely. When Rachael was ready for the hike, she called over to Buck and said, smiling, "Don't forget the sat phone; ever since we moved here you have been so forgetful."

Buck looked at her. "And you love me anyway."

As Buck picked up his bag to carry up the mountain, the local guide started up the trail. With Buck and Rachael following the guide, they made good time for the first two hours of the hike. After stopping to rest, the guide went ahead of them a little ways. He then came back down and motioned to follow him into the jungle. After getting off the trail a short distance away, they could hear voices coming down the trail. As they sat there in the brush, both Buck and Rachael brought their pistols out to be ready for whatever would happen next. As the voices got closer, Buck recognized one of the shapes as they made their way down the trail. It was Miguel, who was being pushed to stay in front of the three men following him. Both realized that Miguel was being forced to take the men to the village below. Buck looked at Rachael and Rachael nodded in agreement. Three shots rang out and the three men fell to the ground. Miguel sat there, stunned by how fast everything had happened. Buck went and checked each one of the men lying on the ground while Rachael went over to Miguel, untying his hands. Miguel looked at Rachael, surprised that she was there.

"How did you know we were coming?" Miguel asked.

"We didn't; we were headed up the mountain to try and make a phone call. What are you doing here?" Rachael asked.

"The bad guys came to our hotel and started beating my cousin for letting the Americans use his vehicles. In order for them to stop beating my cousin, I agreed to take them to you, hoping I could escape and warn you that they were coming."

"Are there anymore at the hotel?" asked Buck as he made his way over to Rachael and Miguel.

"They left two down at the hotel to watch over my cousin and his family."

The guide started rummaging through the dead men's clothes, looking for anything of value. He found a pocketknife in one pair of pants, which made him smile. And he found some papers and pictures in the other man's shirt pocket, which he brought over to Buck. Pointing at the picture and then pointing at Buck, Buck looked at the picture and immediately realized that it was a picture of him and Rachael. Buck handed the picture to Rachael who, after looking at it, was just as surprised as Buck was.

"How did they get this picture of us and who took it?" Buck asked.

Rachael studied the picture for a minute and handed it back to Buck. "Look at the clothes we're wearing in the picture and look at the background."

Buck studied it a little closer and realized the picture of them was while they were in Miami Beach. And the clothes they had on were what they were wearing when they had lunch with Evans and Linda.

"Could it be Rasmussen was following us?" asked Rachael.

"I don't know, and at this point I don't know who we can trust, period."

Rachael asked the guide for the paperwork that he had found. The guide gave it to her and left to look for some more. The papers were written in Spanish and neither Buck nor Rachael could read them. They looked at Miguel and asked if he knew how to read. Miguel smiled, "I am a very good reader, I went to school for seven years, learned how to read very well."

Buck handed the paperwork over to Miguel and asked him to read it for them. Miguel looked at the paperwork and looked at Buck and Rachael. "It says here you are wanted by the cartel and that they offer a reward for your capture."

"Who is willing to pay the reward?" asked Rachael.

Miguel read a little farther and then went to the next page, reading it. Miguel replied, "U.S. Government will pay for you to be captured."

At that statement, both of them sat down on the ground and waited for the shock to wear off. Buck was the first to speak. "We need to talk to Evans and Linda to find out what's going on."

Rachael looked at Miguel. "Any more of these guys up the trail?"

Miguel shook his head no. Buck looked at the guide, "Are you willing to take us to the top of the mountain?"

The guide shook his head yes and started up the mountain again.

"I will go with you, too," Miguel said.

After getting rid of the bodies and getting their weapons, Buck and Rachael started the hike again. When they reached the summit, Buck called out on the sat phone and was able to talk to Evans.

"Where have you two been?" Evans asked.

"We've been hiding out and waiting to talk to you. We just got word that our government has us listed as fugitives; do you know anything about this?"

Evans cussed under his breath, "Let me look into it. I swear I know nothing about this. Man, how many leaks we got here in this building? Were you able to get the old couple out of the safe house?"

"Yes, we were," looking at Miguel to explain.

"Yes, they are fine; we hide them when we found out about the men looking for you," Miguel replied.

"Evans, they are fine."

"That's good, I'll contact the army and have Captain Rich and his team pick you up before they leave the area down there."

"Good, find out what's going on and why we are wanted by the cartel, as well as our own government."

"I'm on it and I will call you as soon as I find out."

At that point, the phone went dead and Buck looked at Rachael. "What do we do now?"

"We go after the men holding Miguel's cousin hostage and make sure the old people are safe."

"Now its war and we don't even know which side we're on."

"That's the easy part; we're on our own side."

After telling the guide goodbye and thanks, Buck and Rachael went with Miguel back down the mountain to the hotel, where the cousin was being held hostage. In two hours, they were standing on the street, where they could see the hotel. The front of it was lit up and as they made their way, staying in the shadows, they could see the guards inside. Buck could tell that they had been drinking and the cousin was in a chair next to them with two black eyes and a busted lip.

Rachael, looking at Miguel, asked, "Is there another way into the hotel?"

Miguel nodded. "Follow me."

Rachael stayed where she was and Buck followed Miguel through the alley- way. Once on the back side of the hotel, Miguel opened the door and led Buck through the garage, where the vehicles were. Miguel showed Buck the door to the hotel from the garage. Buck moved up to the door, cracking it open to see if anything was on the other side. Seeing nothing, he went through the door and made his way to the front of the hotel via the kitchen. After crossing the kitchen into the main lobby, he could see the two guards standing there, drinking their tequila, and moved ever closer.

By now Rachael could see into the hotel lobby and could see Buck moving in; she did the same. Buck fired once and took the guard out closest to him and Rachael shot the other guard from the front of the hotel. As both men lay on the floor, the cousin, who had been sitting, stood up and kicked one of the dead men and spit on him, cussing him out, calling him names. When Buck had come out from the back of the kitchen, the cousin ran over and gave him a hug. By then Rachael came through the front door and stood over the bodies. She knelt down and started going through the pockets of the dead men, looking for whatever she could find. She found nothing of value on either of them and walked over to where Buck was standing with the cousin and Miguel.

Rachael put her gun away into her holster. "Pretty good shooting for a man."

Buck looked at her. "Aw shucks, 'tweren't nothing, ma'am."

They both laughed at this and checked the cousin for any damage done to him. The cousin was so happy that Buck and

Rachael had returned to kill the two men he was jumping all around the place. The cousin told his family to get the bodies of the two men out of the lobby and take them where they wouldn't be found by anyone. The older boys did as their dad directed them to do.

Miguel started talking to the cousin, and after few minutes Miguel walked over to Buck. "Buck, my cousin says these two men were looking for you because of the taking of the old couple from the safe house in Bogota'. Now he says that one of the men who was guarding the old couple was a son of the kingpin. Make kingpin look bad if son is dead and Americans are to blame. He filed a complaint to State Department for the murder of his son, saying Americans murdered him for no reason."

Buck looked at Rachael. "Now it all makes sense."

Rachael shook her head in agreement. "Using our own system against us."

Buck looked at Miguel, "Would you be willing to come to America and testify in our behalf, if needed?"

"Yes, when do we leave for America?"

Buck looked at Rachael. "We need to talk to Evans again."

"I agree, to let him know what we know."

Buck pulled out the sat phone and dialed Evans' phone number again. On the second ring Evans picked up the phone. "What's up?"

As Buck was talking to Evans, he walked into the kitchen area for some privacy. In about 10 minutes Buck reappeared and the look on his face was one of relief. Rachael could see the difference in his face and walked over to him, "Well, what happened?"

"The hunt by our government is called off for two reasons. First of all, Evans called the State Department here in Colombia and explained what was going on with us and that they caught the kingpin. He is in a maximum-security prison in the states and, accordingly, he has no political clout with the State Department or the Colombian political structure anymore."

Rachael let out a big sigh of relief. "Thank you for that."

"And a big amen from the choir member," said Buck.

"What do we do now?"

"Well it's like this--we aren't out of the woods yet. We still have the cartel coming after us, and they will keep coming until we get back to the states. That's the easy part. Now they want us to work with the captain and his men to find the DEA agent that no one has heard from for a while. Also, he wants us to work with the captain and his men to try and locate the signals from the computers that were bugged with that e-mail virus that was sent via the FBI office in

Miami. The U.S. Air Force is sending one of their Pave lows down here to assist us in tracking the computers. We are to meet the captain and his team at the airport and be picked up by a C-130 aircraft, possibly the same one that brought us down here."

It took a minute for Rachael to digest all that Buck had said. "My greatest concern about all of this is, will we get frequent-flyer miles for this?"

Buck looked at her and smiled. "That's my girl, always looking for a free trip to South America and mileage as well. Now I know why I married you."

The next day the sun rose just the same as it had the day before, and the sky was blue with clouds slowly moving towards the inland with a gentle breeze pushing them along. Buck and Rachael woke up in a bed for the first time in days, and it felt good, even if it had bedbugs in it. They came down the stairway, making their way to the kitchen for some coffee and maybe some breakfast.

Miguel was there, smiling. "Did you sleep good last night?"

"It was like heaven," Buck and Rachael replied.

Miguel followed them into the kitchen. "Do we leave for America today?"

Buck looked at him and then at Rachael. "We're not leaving for America today. My boss wants us to stay here in Colombia and help the army find some more bad people."

At this, Miguel bowed his head and said nothing.

Rachael then said, reassuringly, "When we get done with catching the bad men, we'll come and get you to go with us to America."

Buck, surprised at what she had just said, looked at her and swallowed hard. "Yes, we will come back and get you."

Miguel, upon hearing this, raised his head and smiled elatedly. "You won't be sorry for this; I will be a great American, wait you see."

Buck looked at him. "It may be some time before we get back, but we'll bring you to America; we promise."

"I will wait until you come back; you won't be sorry."

He took off and went to do some of the chores that needed to be done.

Rachael looked at Buck. "How can we say no to a boy that saved our lives a couple of times while we've been down here?"

Buck thought about it and agreed with her.

After breakfast was over, Buck and Rachael headed to the airport with Miguel in the back of the Ford Explorer so that he could take it back to the cousin. Miguel stayed with them until the C-130 taxied to the flight line. The back opened up and the captain came out to greet them. "Long time no see; you been having fun without me here in the sun and jungle?"

Buck replied, as they made their way to the plane, "Couldn't have asked for a better vacation."

Stopping halfway, both Buck and Rachael turned around and went back to where Miguel was standing with tears in his eyes. Buck, speaking first, said, "We will be back to get you."

Rachael gave the boy a hug. "We love you and will miss you till we come and get you."

Miguel hugged both of them and finally let go. The captain came back and asked, "What's up?"

Buck explained what Miguel had done for them and how he saved their lives a couple of times in the jungle. The captain looked at Miguel. "You like to fly?"

"I don't know, I have never been flying before."

The captain, smiling, asked, "Would you like to fly with us?"

Miguel's eyes widened in disbelief. "Can I?"

"Why not, come on--we're burning daylight."

With that, Miguel became an American on that day. All four of them boarded the C-130 and the plane took off and headed to Panama to pick up the helicopter from the Air Force. Miguel would fly on the C-130 to

Miami and land at the Air Force Reserve Base, where he would be met by Evans and Linda, with whom he would stay until Buck and Rachael returned.

CHAPTER XIV

After landing in Panama to pick up the helicopter, Buck and Rachael said goodbye a second time to Miguel. All were happy, knowing that at the end of the mission they would be together forever. After talking to the flight crew about Miguel the loadmaster said he would take care of Miguel and make sure he got to Evans and Linda when they landed in Florida.

While flying from Panama, Miguel was able to go up into the cockpit and see the view the pilot and copilot had from their seats. Miguel was like a kid in a candy shop, asking questions and looking out the windows of the aircraft, looking at the Doppler radar system and all of the instruments on the pancl while the flight engineer explained all of it to him. For Miguel, this experience was the beginning of so many yet to come in a place that was so different from the jungles he grew up in. Only in time would Miguel grow to understand that even freedom in a new country comes at a price that everybody must pay to appreciate the blessings therein. But for now, the adventure was about to begin for him, and he was enjoying it.

Rachael and Buck talked to the captain about the new mission they were about to start, showing him, the computer and paperwork found in the safe house in Bogota'.

The captain called the sergeant over. "Who on our team is the computer guru?"

"That would be Collins with the electronic gear. The kid's crazy about that stuff."

Buck walked over to where Collins was sitting and introduced himself. Buck explained about finding the computer at the safe house in Bogota' and how they couldn't break into it to find what was on it. "Do you think you can open it and see what's on the computer?" Buck asked.

Collins looked at the laptop. "I should know in about hour what's on it."

Buck left Collins and walked back to where Rachael was and sat down. He looked at Rachael, "Collins thinks he can have something in about an hour."

Buck shook his head and let out a sigh. Rachael looked at him. "What was that all about?"

"The kids like Collins make me feel old. They're more computer savvy and smarter than I'll ever be."

Rachael put her hand in his and squeezed it, saying, "Yeah, they may be smarter but you're sexier in your bathing suit."

Buck laughed. "So, you think he is smarter than I am?"

"You know he may be smarter than you, but you're still sexier and I love my men in sheriffs' uniforms. There is something about a man wearing a badge that really gets to me." Rachael laughed.

Buck started to blush. "I bet you say that to all of the policemen."

"Just the one I love, and that one is you." She laughed.

Buck leaned over and kissed her. "So, you go for the older types, do you?"

"Not that old, but you'll do."

The captain had the sergeant gather everybody around. "The Air Force was kind enough to send us a state-of-the-art helicopter and crew to fly us around looking for more of the computers with the virus on it in hopes we can catch some bad guys. The Director of the FBI was happy with our latest catch and thought we would be able to do more with better equipment on hand. Hence, the U.S. Air Force will be flying us in and out of the areas where we pick up the signals. The goal of this mission is to shut down one of the biggest cartels operating in South America, Mexico, and the U.S. Any questions?" No hands went up, and the sergeant looked at the men and said, "This being summer and with the new mission coming on, we should be home by Christmas of next year."

The men laughed and all of them shouted, "Hoo-ah."

With the speech done, the captain turned the men over to the sergeant to get them on the Air Force helicopter. The Pave low helicopter was state-of-the-art for electronics, distance and payload capability, going farther and carrying more than the standard helicopter or its predecessor. The electronics on board were the best in show in the electronics world with most of it being classified, thus making its full potential unknown to the world. The Pave lows are considered to be the Cadillacs in the sky for comfort and durability and for getting into tight spots and coming out on the other end unscathed.

When the helicopter was loaded with all the equipment and the team, it lifted off the pad and headed back into Colombia.

Collins came over to Buck. "I was able to get into the computer and this is what I found inside."

Buck looked at the screen, "Thank you, Collins."

As Buck and Rachael looked at the computer screen, most of it was coded but the fragments that were legible helped piece together a layout of the same kind of network used by the cartel. Buck showed the information to the captain and asked, "Does any of this make sense to you?"

The captain looked at it. "Clear as mud to me; how about we give the flyboys a chance at it."

Buck and the captain went to the wizzo and showed him the computer. The wizzo looked it over. "I've got an idea for this." He hooked the laptop computer up to the master computer on board the helicopter and downloaded the memory on the hard drive of the laptop to the master computer. After a couple of minutes, the screen on the master computer showed what had been on the laptop. A few clicks on the computer keyboard and the gibberish on the screen turned into English, then all of it was readable. The wizzo looked at the guys who were amazed at what just happened. "Don't ask or I'll have to shoot you."

"Can you reload it onto the laptop in English so we can study it for a while?" the captain asked.

The wizzo clicked a few more keys and the information was back on the laptop in English. With that accomplished, the captain and Buck went back to their seats and settled down as Buck and Rachael started looking over the material on the laptop.

The information gave a list of names and places where the e-mails were being sent after being reviewed, plus a listing of e-mails received from the others that had not been opened yet. After thinking for a moment, Buck went back to the wizzo. "Can you send the stuff on this computer to the FBI office in Miami?"

"I sure can; just give me an address and it's done," The wizzo said.

Buck called Evans on the sat phone and explained what he wanted to do. Evans called his IT section and asked for a safe address to have the material sent to, and within minutes the material was sent to that address in the IT section of the FBI. The list of the e-mail titles that had been on the laptop would all have an origination source to track. All of the opened and unopened e-mails were using aliases to further protect themselves in case somebody hacked their system. This would not make a difference to the IT team. The origination source would eventually identify who and where they were. The IT team in Miami was going to have a field day with the e-mail addresses and names of people and places that would be found. The IT team asked for a white board to use in building the structure of the cartel and its span of control. The goal was to create the organizational structure of the cartel and show where the money went, the people involved, and the dummy corporations used to launder the money back to the cartel, as well as the setup of the distributors in the U.S. With this organizational structure in place, the network could be brought down or monitored by the FBI. All of this from a simple computer e-mail hack.

With this information having been sent to Miami, Buck went back and sat down next to Rachael again and tried to sleep a little.

The rest of the flight was quiet. After they landed at the airport in Bogota' the men got out of the helicopter to stretch their legs and to move around a little bit while the helicopter was being refueled. For Buck and Rachael, it felt good to get out of the cramped space inside the helicopter and feel the sun. The captain came over to them. "Do you think the signal on the laptop can be loaded onto the computer the Air Force has inside the helicopter? I was thinking, with the signal frequency loaded onto the Air Force computer, their system would be looking in a bigger area for the signal."

"And with the IT people in Miami working on the information from the laptop, they could direct us to the important places and people to look for without wasting our time and energy on the stuff that didn't matter," Buck added.

The captain thought for a moment. "Who knows, we might be home for Christmas this year." Buck and the captain laughed at this, knowing there may be some truth in the statement.

After the helicopter had been refueled and was ready to go again, the men loaded back onto the helicopter and readied themselves for another flight. Buck and Rachael joined them, along with the captain. The helicopter took off again and headed into the mountains. At this point of the trip the flight crew was looking for a place to set down on a mountaintop and basically sit and wait for a signal to appear. Waiting allowed the IT team to do their magic and give the team directions to find a target. After studying the satellite photos of the surrounding area, they found a mountaintop to set down on. This became a base camp for the team while they waited. The soldiers proceeded under the direction of the sergeant to set up their tents and break out the MRE's for lunch.

As they were sitting on top of the mountain eating, Buck looked at Rachael. "So how long do we keep doing this?"

Rachael looked at him. "Until we are ready to go."

Buck sat there for a moment and thought about all that they had been through of late. "I guess we should see where the computer e-mails take us."

"It was our idea to do it."

At this point, the captain came up and sat down next to Buck and Rachael, eating his MRE's, not saying a word. Buck looked at him and asked, "So why are you doing this, Captain?"

"Doing what?"

"Chasing these drug people and burning the farms?"

"Well for me, it's pretty simple. I had a brother who was older than me, loved to play sports and was considered a jock by all the kids in school. Being the little brother, I idolized him; I wanted to be like him in every way possible. He was in the cool kid's crowd, and with the cool kids they got into drinking and drugs. However, he couldn't handle it. One night while out with his friends, he overdosed on the drugs and was rushed to the hospital, where he never regained consciousness. I watched what it did to my parents, nearly tearing them to pieces. My mom never fully recovered from it. My dad, who was so proud of him, was devastated by his death. The toxicology report said that he had used enough drugs to kill a horse, as it was; he stood no chance of surviving. I went looking for the person who sold the drugs to my brother, and when I found him I beat him up so bad that he's in a wheelchair for the rest of his life in a home for invalids. They never found out who gave him the beating, and when I was old enough, I went to college and became an officer so that I could work in the counter drugs unit." He looked at Buck and Rachael and said without blinking, "I should've killed him. Well, from that time forward I decided I would try and stop it wherever and whenever I could."

Buck and Rachael sat there in silence and continued eating their food without saying a word. By then the sergeant came over and said, "The wizzo would like to talk to you three."

With that, the three set their food down and walked over to where the wizzo was standing.

"You wanted to see us," The captain said.

The wizzo turned around and looked at them. "Those IT guys in Miami must be working overtime on what we sent them. They sent a message to us stating they have a target for us to go after in Bogota' near the capitol building. Evidently, the person of interest is a big player in the drug business. He ships the drugs from the golden triangle in Southeast Asia to supplement what they grow here in Colombia to meet the demand in the U.S."

"Who is he?" the captain asked.

"I'll do one even better than that--here is his picture," the wizzo said.

Buck and Rachael looked at the picture. "What's his name?"

The wizzo came back with a chuckle, "Ernesto Johann Smith."

"This guy was to be our contact if we got into trouble down here," Buck said as he looked at Rachael.

"The message sent to us said to terminate with prejudice," the wizzo replied.

"What does 'terminate with prejudice' mean, Captain?" Buck asked the captain.

"We are to kill him."

With that, the captain called out to the sergeant, "Sergeant, get the men ready."

Rachael looked at Buck. "I guess the FBI doesn't like being made fools of."

The sergeant had the men ready to go in short order, and the captain went to the men and explained what the mission was. "For this we cannot be dressed in military clothes; we need to look like civilians."

Pointing to Buck and Rachael, the captain said, "These two will be the lead on this mission. Their job will be to get in and get out quickly. We will back them up to make sure they can do their part."

Buck and Rachael looked at each other and smiled. "And the fun keeps coming our way," Buck said.

"Since I've done this before, I will take the lead, if you wish," Rachael said.

"With you in front, I'll follow you anywhere," Buck said, smiling at her.

Rachael smacked him and giggled a little. "Men!"

The captain looked at the wizzo. "Do we have any more information on our target?"

The wizzo looked at the message. "He can be found at this address: Carrera 7 No. 116 - 05. It's in the north part of town, past the business district," he said, handing the message to the captain, who in turn handed it to Buck and Rachael.

"From my understanding, there is a CATAM military airport that we can land at if you want to go that way," the captain said.

The flight crew thought about flying to the base, and the pilot responded, "It would be easier for us to exit when needed."

The captain, looking at the sergeant, asked, "How far away are we from Bogota' right now?"

"As the crow flies, we are about 10 clicks away."

The captain thought for a minute. "How about you flyboys take us to the outskirts of town and we'll hoof it from there?"

The pilot looked at the maps and suggested, "How about we drop you guys off here and wait for you at the same place?"

"That will be fine and we'll leave you two men for security in case anything happens before we get back," the captain said.

The pilot nodded in agreement and started plotting the flight.

"If we go in at night, the men will not need to go civilian," the sergeant said.

"In their uniforms, they may blend in well if something goes wrong," the captain agreed.

After the planning was done, the team got ready to move the helicopter. They started the propellers swinging through the air and the engines whining to full power. The flight crew took their positions. All but two of the team, who were left to guard the base camp, loaded onto the helicopter.

The helicopter lifted off the top of the mountain at 7:00 pm. With darkness falling fast, they would be invisible to the prying eyes of the curious. When the helicopter landed at the exact place they had agreed upon, the team, with the captain out front, unloaded out of the helicopter. The captain signaled his men to form a perimeter around the helicopter until everybody was set. The pilot and copilot had night-vision goggles and used them to look the area over, to be safe. The sergeant gathered the men together and, looking at his map and the GPS coordinates, pointed in the direction they needed to go. Again, leaving two men behind for security, the captain took the lead with a point man 20 yards up the road.

Buck and Rachael were in the center of the group as they left to find their way to the target. The distance from where they had landed to where the house was, was about five miles, an easy walk for the team on the streets. They moved quietly, and when they ran into trouble with the locals thinking they were easy targets to mug at night, the team would massage the would-be mugger's face with their SAWs. They would go down and the men would drag their bodies over into an alleyway. They made it to the house in about an hour. Standing across the street in a dark alley, the captain was trying to figure how to get in without being detected.

Rachael and Buck looked it over and Buck said, "I got an idea, how about we

just knock on the door and tell Ernesto we need his help in getting out of Bogota' because the cartel men are after us."

The captain thought about it for a minute. "That might work, especially if he thinks that he can hold you inside the house. My men will sneak in through the window right there," pointing to the window on the first floor, "and I'll follow you in once he opens the door."

Buck looked at him, "Sounds like a plan to me."

"You said I could lead the way on this one, at least let me knock on the door first." Rachael smiled.

Buck and the captain chuckled. "If you're real nice all the way up to the door, I'll let you knock on it first."

Rachael, still smiling, said, "Oh, goody, goody."

The captain motioned for the sergeant to take his men over to the window and, using his hands, signaled to break into the house. Buck and Rachael walked over to the house with the captain following about three feet behind them, watching their rear. Rachael knocked on the door and waited for some kind of movement inside. She knocked again; this time a light came on and she heard a voice saying, "Who is it?"

"I'm Rachael and my husband, who's been shot, needs your help quickly," Rachael replied.

With that, the door opened and the man standing there asked, "Who are you again?"

Rachael explained, "We are from America. We were sent here by the FBI and we were told that if we ran into any trouble, we should contact you."

The man looked around out into the street. "Come on in."

When Rachael and Buck walked in, the captain followed from behind, saying, "Old man, find a chair to sit on."

The old man was surprised by all of this and started to get upset. "Who do you think you are, barging into my home like this?"

The captain looked at him. "Shut up or I'll kill you now."

Seeing the intensity in the captain's face, the old man sat down without a word. At this point Buck asked, "Old man, where do you keep your business computer?"

The old man pointed to the other room, and the captain headed that way. By now the rest of the team walked into where the old man was sitting and stood there looking at him. The sergeant sent two men to search the house for people and or anything of Intel value. After they took off, the old man asked, "Why are you here in my home?"

Buck looked at Rachael as she said, "We found out you are working both sides of the fence here. You're receiving drugs from Southeast Asia and selling them to the cartel, while you're supposed to be helping the FBI and DEA with the drug issues here in Colombia."

The old man smiled and laughed at Rachael. "You Americans are fools to think I would work for you, betraying my people, and sell myself to you."

The captain came through the door from the room he had been in, carrying a laptop and some papers he had found. Handing them off to one of the soldiers, he stood there listening to the old man talk. The captain asked the old man, "How many of your own people have you killed getting rich from the drugs you ship in from Asia?"

The old man looked at the captain, "I have killed none of my people."

"How about the people who stand up to you for selling drugs in Colombia and doing business that kills the people in other countries like Mexico and the U.S.?" the captain asked.

The man sat there for a moment and answered, "They are not my people; what happens to them in their country is their business."

With that, the captain pulled his semi-auto out and asked the old man, "Do you have anything else to say?"

The old man, realizing he was about to die, said, "What about my family? They'll be heartbroken."

The captain asked the old man, "What about the families of the dead people who tried to stand up against the cartel which you took money from on your drug sales?"

The old man sat there, speechless for a moment, then said, "Get on with it."

The captain fired twice with both shots to the head and the old man slumped in the chair. The captain, looking for the sergeant, said, "Lets' go; we're done here."

The men, with Buck and Rachael, left the house through the front door, turning out the lights and slipping into the shadows on the street.

As Buck and Rachael reviewed what had happened in the house, they started talking about it. Rachael said, "Greed at any cost comes with a price. I guess you got to be able to pay for it when it comes time. If you can't afford it, you need to rethink if it's worth it."

"I don't understand how people can rationalize their actions with other people dying in the process for them to be rich and comfortable," Buck agreed.

Rachael looked at Buck. "They got to have a heart first to feel for others, and these people don't, at least for the ones they don't know."

The rest of the way was quiet and as they made their way through the streets of Bogota', there was an eerie silence in the city. When they arrived at the helicopter, the flight crew was sitting there, playing cards. The captain came in and asked the wizzo to send a message back to the FBI, saying target terminated. At that, the pilot and copilot started the Pave low as the team climbed aboard and they headed back to their base camp up on the mountain. The captain asked the sergeant to give the laptop he had taken from the house to the wizzo to transfer the information on the hard drive to the FBI in Miami. Once the wizzo accomplished the transfer of information and had received a confirmation reply, he let the sergeant know, who in turn told the captain it was complete. The captain closed his eyes and dozed till they landed on the hilltop. When the helicopter landed at the base camp, the men were ready for bed, and all of them made their way to the pup tents and lay down and slept. Buck and Rachael stayed aboard the helicopter, sleeping on the floor. Both were asleep in a matter of seconds, and the only ones awake were the guards, who kept an eye over their team for safety and security.

The next morning Buck and Rachael woke to the noise of the men cleaning up the camp and putting away their tents. Buck went out to find the captain and upon finding him asked, "What's up?"

"We have a new target in another part of Colombia. We also got word from the FBI about the download we sent last night. The FBI says that the information regarding the business dealings of Ernesto shows a trail all the way back to Southeast Asia--names and places and points of contact in Colombia and other parts of Nicaragua, showing the route, the drugs take from point A to point B. The hard drive also showed his contacts in the cartel who he did business with in selling the drugs."

Buck looked at him. "We keep this up, we'll never get home."

The captain agreed, saying, "The target we're going after now is one they found on the hard drive last night. He's living in Medellin in the suburbs of El Poblado on the northeastern edge of the city. Our target's name is Mateo Diaz, he is the main trafficker of the drugs to Mexico from Colombia. Mateo would buy the drugs from Ernesto and deliver the drugs via truck and boat to Mexico to the cartel. The final shipments would be sent from Mexico to the U.S."

After breakfast, the team had reloaded the helicopter with their gear and started boarding for their next flight. The trip would be a short one-hour hop to Medellin. This time, they would be landing in the daylight and their helicopter could be seen by the locals in the area. The pilot and copilot decided to land a little further away from the city in order to keep the helicopter from being a target. This meant the team would have to hike into the city from a longer distance in order to protect the helicopter.

Buck was looking at the clothes he had on and noticed they were not as tight-fitting as they used to be. Rachael was watching this from a distance and said, "Looks like living in South America agrees with you."

"You too, as well. It must be the mountain air."

"It could be just the mountains we've been climbing up and down."

"I think you're right on that one. Come on, we better hurry; we don't want them waiting for the two-old people on the tea," said Buck.

After getting situated, the team started down the mountain with the captain in the lead once more. Leaving the helicopter with the normal two soldiers for security, the point man was about 30 yards in front of the main group with one soldier for the rear guard as they threaded their way through the jungle. In their travel down the mountain they came across an old village that had the bones of the dead strewn around the place. Some of the skeletons had broken bones, while others had holes in their skulls. Everyone stopped to look around the village. Buck and Rachael were looking around as well, noticing the holes in the skulls.

"Do you know what had happened here?" Buck asked the captain.

"It looks like another tribe of people hostile to this village came in and wiped it out."

Rachael, looking around said, "Tribal warfare so close to the cities?"

"Yet it's not enough to be part of the drug culture. Sometimes you wipe out the competition of other workers for more of the jobs and money for your own village," the captain replied.

After looking around the remains of the village and finding nothing of value, the team continued on their way. Buck and Rachael were able to keep up with the team and didn't need to take as many breaks. The point man found a foot trail down the mountain about 10 yards away from where the team was. After notifying the captain about the trail, the captain decided to take it, making the trek a little easier.

By the afternoon they were standing on one of the mountains overlooking the city of

Medellin. Their trek through the jungle had put them within five miles of the city. They decided to rest here while waiting for the darkness to settle in before moving on.

After sunset, the team was up and ready to head into town. Once again, Buck and Rachael would be in the lead with the captain as they made their way to the city, hiking the last five miles to town. With nightfall coming fast, the team snaked their way into the city. Buck and Rachael looked at the surroundings of the city and noticed that this part of the city was modern and looked like a regular suburb of Phoenix. This made traveling here especially hard because the nightlife was everywhere. The lights of the city were a stark contrast to being on the mountaintop near Bogota'. Traveling through the city by the alleyway was not an easy task, and it took extra time not to be seen. When they found the address to the house they were looking for, they confirmed it with their GPS. Once done, the captain had his team setup a perimeter around the house and secure it.

The captain looked at Buck and Rachael and said, "I don't think knocking on the door is going to work this time. Besides, it looks as if he may not be home yet."

Buck and Rachael nodded in agreement, with Rachael saying, "If that's the case, let's go inside and make ourselves at home and wait for him."

The captain looked around and, finding the sergeant, said, "Collins, come up and go inside with us."

The sergeant called for Collins and told him to follow the captain. After breaking into the house and disabling the house alarm, the captain told Collins, "I need you to find the laptop and do your magic on it and see if you can open it up to get the hard drive downloaded."

Collins nodded his head and started looking for the computer. Rachael and Buck started going through each one of the rooms, clearing the house to make sure no one was there. The captain stayed by the door, just in case Mateo came home.

After Buck and Rachael were done clearing the rooms, they met the captain in the front of the house. Collins had showed up already with the laptop and he and the captain were going through the hard drive, trying to find anything useful on it. Buck, looking over their shoulders, noticed an address kept showing up on the screen with numbers in kilos. Rachael was watching as well, and all of a sudden Rachael had an idea about the kilo numbers and the address.

Rachael looked at Buck and chuckled. "Do you think that this address maybe where he keeps his drugs before being shipped out and the kilo numbers are the amount he has inside the warehouse on a daily basis?"

"Well, duh, why didn't I think of that?" the captain said.

Buck looked at Rachael. "I love it when a lady takes command of the situation."

With that, the captain fed the address into the GPS to see where the address was in reference to Mateo's house. After a minute or two the map showed up on the system, saying it was a half mile from where they were.

The captain looked at Buck and Rachael. "Are you up for another walk on the wild side?"

Rachael looked at him, "Oh, Captain, the things you say to the party crowd."

"Collins, you take the computer and head out. Tell the sergeant to get all but two of the men ready to move out. Have the two men stay behind for security in case we miss Mateo at the warehouse," the captain said.

A few minutes later the team was ready to move out. The captain walked over to the two men who were to be security and said, "Make sure if Mateo shows up he is taken out."

The two men nodded and went back into the shadows of the alleyway. The captain had the sergeant lead the way this time, with Buck and Rachael in the lead as well. A half hour later they were standing in front of the warehouse. The sergeant and the captain went a little closer to look inside to see what was going on. After looking inside the building they could see people moving loaded pallets to where trucks were parked. As they reached the building, the captain saw that there were two guards at the front door. Carefully moving around them, they made their way to the back side of the building. From where they were they could see men loading a truck with pallets of sealed bags in the shape of thick bricks. The captain, using his binoculars, watched the pallets get loaded onto the truck and noticed there were two other trucks waiting to be loaded. The captain handed the binoculars to the sergeant, who watched the activities below and after a minute handed the binoculars back to the captain, saying, "My, my, my, those guys are pretty busy down there."

The captain smiled. "Did you see any guards down there?"

"None that I could see."

The sergeant and the captain made their way back to where the team was waiting. The captain explained, "They're loading the trucks with pallets with what looks to be sealed bags of drugs. I'm thinking we can go through the front door and walk to the back, where the staging area is, and take them out."

"I have an idea; why don't we let them load the trucks with the pallets and hijack the trucks before they leave the warehouse? That way we get the drugs and the trucks," the sergeant said.

Buck chuckled and Rachael laughed, saying, "Sergeant, you have such a devious mind."

The sergeant grinned when he heard that. The captain thought about it and said, "First of all, we need to get rid of the drivers and then hijack the trucks."

With that, the team went towards the front of the building and waited for the two guards to be taken out by the soldiers. The rest of the team made their way into the front of the building and slowly walked into the back of the warehouse. On the way, Buck and Rachael went into the offices in the front of the building to make sure there was no one that could surprise the team. Finding one of the offices had the light on, they went to check it out, telling the captain they'd meet him in a couple of minutes. The captain looked at Buck. "Don't be late; you don't want to miss your ride."

Buck looked at him and laughed, "We'll be there."

As Buck and Rachael proceeded down the hallway to where the light was on, they could hear a voice talking on a phone. As they inched closer to the door of the office, they looked inside. Sitting at the desk was

Mateo. He was talking and hadn't noticed that Buck and Rachael were outside his door. After closing out his conversation and hanging up, he started to get up to leave the office. As he made his way to the door, he was met by Buck. Mateo, surprised by Buck, stood there not knowing what to do.

Mateo looked at him and, regaining his composure, said, "What are you doing in here? How did you get by my guards?"

Buck looked at him and said, "What guards? Oh, you mean the dead ones?"

This upset Mateo and he started to call for his men. Rachael came in from the other side of the door and smacked him in the head. Rachael looked at Buck. "He talks too much."

They dragged Mateo to the back of the building, where they found the team slowly but methodically gathering up the workers and drivers and putting them into a locked room. With the trucks fully loaded and ready to roll, the sergeant ordered the soldiers to standby until the demolition team was able to do their job. They put Mateo in the back of the second truck, with Buck and Rachael providing security. The captain and the sergeant were in the lead truck, waiting for the demolitions to be planted and the timers to be set for thirty minutes. When the demolition team finished and came running to get in the trucks, the captain yelled, "Let's get out of here."

As the trucks wound through the city, the soldiers in the back of the trucks started opening the bags on the pallets and started dumping the drugs onto the streets. At one place, they found a manhole cover, which they opened, and poured the drugs down into the sewer. By the time they made it to the outskirts of the city, they crossed a bridge, where they dumped the rest of the drugs into the river. As they continued driving, they could see a faint glow over the city where the warehouse had been. The glow lit up the city as a warm spot in the sky. Before disabling the trucks, they made their way back to the house to pick up the two soldiers left behind and continued their trek back to the helicopter.

With Mateo with them, they hiked to where the helicopter was, reaching it just before sunrise. They pointed out to Mateo the faint glow in the sky. "You see that faint glow over there?" asked the captain.

Mateo looked and nodded yes, to which the captain explained with satisfaction, "That, my friend, is your warehouse going up in flames."

Buck looked at Mateo. "Looks as if you are out of business now and, by the way, your drugs are gone as well."

Mateo looked at the captain and Buck. "I'm going to kill you for what you've done."

"What should we do with him now, Captain?" The sergeant asked.

The captain looked at the sergeant. "We have our orders, Sergeant."

By now Mateo knew he was about to die, and yelled, "Wait, wait, what do you want to know? I will tell you!"

Rachael looked at the captain. "He may be worth more to us alive than dead right now."

The captain looked at Mateo and asked, "What do you know that would make us not kill you?"

"I know the contacts that are in the city government in Medellin and in Mexico so that we are not bothered by police," Mateo offered.

"In about five minutes they will be useless to us and to you," the captain said.

Mateo was sweating now, knowing if he didn't offer anything the captain wanted it would be over for him. Stammering, he said, "I know where the main distribution point is in Mexico and where the drugs are stored until it's time to move them."

That caught the captain by surprise and he turned and looked at Mateo. "You know where there are more drugs?"

Mateo, realizing that this may be his ticket to staying alive, said, "Yes, I will show you where it's at."

The captain looked at Mateo. "You have bought yourself some time, senor."

At that point, the wizzo came over and said, "According to the news on the radio, they just found Ernesto in his home."

"Do the police have any idea who did it?" the captain asked.

"The police are saying a mob hit from one of the cartels," the wizzo replied.

"Good."

The captain then turned to the sergeant. "Bring Mateo over here to look at this map."

Everybody concerned was waiting for Mateo to show them the location of the drug warehouse for the cartel in Mexico. Mateo looked at the captain and asked, "How do I know you won't shoot me after I tell you?"

The captain pulled his semi-auto and, pointing it at him, said, "How about I shoot you now so you won't have to wonder about it anymore?"

With that question answered, Mateo started looking at the map they had laid out. Mateo studied it for a minute and said, "This is the place where they store the drugs."

He stood there, pointing at a dot on the map called Culiacán City in northwestern Mexico. "It is the largest city and the capital of the state of Sinaloa and considered to be the headquarters to the Monterrey Cartel."

The flight crew looked at the surrounding area, and the pilot said, "If we can set up a base camp in the mountains east of the city, then you can walk into the city and do your magic."

Buck and Rachael looked at each other. "Maybe we need to think this over."

The captain looked at them. "Think about what?"

"I know you're not afraid to go, that's understood; however, we'd be walking into a heavily fortified city owned and operated by the cartel. We could possibly get in and blow up the warehouse, but I'm not sure we would be able get out without someone getting hurt in the process," Buck said.

"So what do you suggest?"

"If it's in an area that is isolated, we could have the Air Force come in with a smart bomb and blow it up."

The captain looked at the sergeant. "What do you think, Sergeant?"

"Well, the men have been at it for quite some time and it's starting to show on them. I think this time we need to let someone with the right equipment go after it. If we can locate the building, then we can send the information through the channels and let them get the glory, while we suck our suds and eat hot dogs at the beach."

The captain thought about it for a moment, looked at his men, and then looked at Mateo. "If I get you the satellite photos of the area of Culiacán City, would you be able to identify where the building is?"

"I will try."

With that, the captain looked at the wizzo and, as he was about to speak, the wizzo said, "Already on it."

In a couple of minutes, the printer on the helicopter started printing Culiacán City in color. Mateo studied the photos and finally located a landmark he recognized and following the street with his finger stopped at a group of buildings on the outskirts of town.

"Here it is," he said.

With that, the captain asked the wizzo for the GPS coordinates for the group of buildings. Once this was done, the captain asked the wizzo to transmit a message to the FBI in Miami about the building being a storage warehouse for the drugs to be sent to the U.S. The wizzo transmitted the information and coordinates to the Miami FBI office and waited for a confirmation. As the captain was talking to the sergeant, the wizzo came over and said, "Message received and new marching orders."

Handing the captain the slip of paper with the orders on it, he read it and handed it to the sergeant. After the sergeant read the orders he said, "Well, here we go again."

Buck and Rachael were given the slip of paper and as they read it they stood there amazed. The message read new signals from e-mail, proceed to Cali for search-and-destroy mission. The flight crew prepped the helicopter and got it ready for flight. The team was packed and ready to go in five minutes, along with Mateo in tow. Buck and Rachael were relieved by the decision of the captain to forego the trip into Mexico. As they made their way to Cali, the electronics-sensors gear the helicopter was carrying started picking up a faint beep. After the wizzo told the captain they had found the signal, the helicopter went into a search pattern, trying to locate the signal. After 10 minutes of searching, the wizzo found the strongest signal next to the river down below. The problem for the helicopter was that it couldn't land because of all the jungle below. After marking the spot for the signal, the helicopter started looking for a place to land. After searching for about 10 minutes, the copilot came back and said, "There is no place to land and we're running low on fuel; what do you want us to do?"

The captain paused a moment. "Drop us off about four clicks from the signal. We'll walk in and call you when we're ready to be picked up."

"Better yet," the pilot said, "we found a small village to the north about two more clicks along the river. If you follow that, that's where will be waiting for you. In the meantime, our bird is thirsty and it needs a drink. How long do you think you'll be in the jungle, Captain?"

"Hard to say at this time, possibly two days, maybe three days at the most."

"In that case, we will see you in two days," said the pilot.

The pilot climbed back into his seat and relayed the conversation to the co-pilot, and in a short amount of time the team, including their guest Mateo, was lowered by ropes into the jungle with Buck and Rachael following them. Within two minutes the sound of the helicopter was gone, and they were all alone in the jungle, as if they had been transported back into prehistoric times.

The sun didn't shine down onto the floor of the jungle because the tree foliage was so thick above and wouldn't allow the sunlight through. With the captain using a compass and GPS as well, they started their trek through the jungle to find the signal and track it. The point man was out about 20 yards this time so he wouldn't lose sight of the team. The rear guard was approximately the same distance. After the first mile, they found a trail and followed it until it split in two directions. Staying close to the coordinates, they took the left fork of the trail. Collins had his headset on listening for the signal. After finding it he notified the sergeant, who relayed the message to the captain. The captain was relieved that they were able to pick up the signal as the jungle was so thick sometimes you felt you were going in circles. The signal would be their guide to get where they needed to be.

The captain told the sergeant, "Have Collins take the lead and we'll follow him to the target."

As Collins made his way to the front of the line, everybody stopped to take a break and catch their breath. Buck lookcd at Rachael, "I'm ready to head back to Arizona after this; how about you?"

"I thought you would never ask."

After a five-minute break, the team started making their way through the jungle once more, with Collins in the front of the line. The captain noticed the river wasn't that far away from where they were. He started thinking that maybe on the way back they could build some rafts and float back, instead of fighting the jungle. After another hour of chopping at the dense foliage of the jungle, Collins reported that the signal was really strong. Taking a break, the captain asked the sergeant to send two men up the trail, scout the area and come back and report.

The two soldiers were sent out and the rest of the team sat and rested, waiting for their return. About an hour later the scouts camc back and reported that they had found a shack near the river and had followed the trail from the shack to a poppy farm, which was about a mile deeper into the jungle. One of the scouts said it wasn't the usual setup that they had seen before in other locations. The captain looked at the scout. "Explain."

Both scouts said the place looked like a staging area for the completed drug packages; however, there was neither a landing strip nor a place to tie up a boat near the shack. There was another trail they found that led off into the jungle, that followed the river. They followed the trail a ways, but not finding anything, they decided to return and report. The captain told the men thanks and asked the sergeant, "How do you want to proceed on this one?"

"First of all, let's get to the shack and check the surrounding area. I get the feeling we're not alone out here. Someone or somebody is following us and has been for a while."

"You got that feeling, too?" asked the captain.

Buck and Rachael started looking around the area themselves but didn't see anything out of the ordinary.

After about 30 minutes of following the trail they arrived at the shack. They then continued following the trail that led from the shack into the jungle. After finding the poppy farm and the buildings, the captain sent more scouts down the trail towards the river. "If you run into something or someone, try and bring it back with you alive, if you can, but don't use your firearms unless you have to."

The scouts nodded their heads and took off through the jungle, following the trail. After securing the area, the captain called the sergeant over. "Look at this setup; have you ever seen anything like this before?"

The sergeant looked around. "It looks like a Walmart center, like a one-stop shopping and delivery service in one place. The question is how the bad guys made the delivery system work."

One of the soldiers called over to the sergeant, "Look what I found, Sergeant." The sergeant walked over to where the soldier was standing and looked at what he had found; it was a piece of rope tied to a boulder. The boulder looked like it had been moved there and had something like a symbol cut into it. Whatever the symbol meant or was, it didn't look like it belonged there. Buck and Rachael walked over to take a look for themselves. Buck looked at the rock and stood there for a moment, saying, "I've seen the symbol on the rock before somewhere else."

By now the captain came over, asking the sergeant, "What's going on?"

After pointing to the rock, the captain stood there a moment, not sure what he was looking at. The captain picked up some soil and spread it across the symbol to highlight it, and that's when Buck remembered where he had seen it before.

"That's it; I knew I'd seen that symbol before."

By now everyone was looking at Buck, wondering what he was talking about. Looking at Rachael, he said, "Remember when we were working the drug case in Phoenix a while back? We found that Mexican mafia guy that had died at the gas station."

Rachael nodded her head and, still trying to make sense of the conversation, asked, "And?"

"One of the tattoos the guy had on his arm was shaped like this one on the rock," Buck continued.

Rachael was trying to recall the man that had died at the gas station that day and still couldn't remember. Buck then said, "I saw it at the warehouse in Medellin on one of the sealed bags of drugs."

The sergeant told the soldier guarding Mateo to bring him over to the boulder. As the soldier led Mateo to the rock, you could tell he recognized the symbol as well. Mateo looked it over for a second or two and stood there, looking at the captain with a look of, what do you want. The captain, looking at Mateo, asked, "Do you know what that symbol is?"

"Yes, I do, it is the symbol for the Monterrey Cartel. They mark all of the bricks with that symbol on the outside of the packages."

"Does it have any other meaning than that?" asked Buck.

"It's used to identify boundaries and other things as to who owns what and where," Mateo replied.

"What does it mean, as far this boulder goes?" the captain asked.

"This area belongs to the Monterrey Cartel and this rock is a kind of off-limits sign to anyone else," Mateo said.

The sergeant looked at the captain and asked, "Why would they need to mark it off limits?"

"Maybe they're hiding something around here," Rachael said.

The captain asked the sergeant to call Collins over super quick. Collins came running over and reported, saying, "You wanted to see me, Sir?"

The captain looked at Collins. "Is your machine still on?"

"No, Sir, I turned it off when we got here, Sir, thinking we found the location of the signal."

The captain looked at the sergeant. "Set up a team with Collins here and start searching the area for that signal again. We know it's here; we need to locate it for real."

The sergeant chose two volunteers to work with Collins. He explained that they were to escort Collins wherever he went with the machine. Collins and his escort started off walking the camp, listening for the signal.

The captain called Buck and Rachael over. "I've been thinking that there are no trails or vehicle tracks leading away from this area. It makes me wonder if this really is a staging area, how would they get the drugs out of here?"

Buck and Rachael looked around at the camp. "I was wondering the same thing, too," Buck replied.

Rachael looked at them for a second. Calling herself dumb for not seeing it sooner, she said, "How about a submarine?"

Buck and the captain both looked at her kind of crazy like, and as they thought about it some more, they looked at her again.

"That's it!" Buck said.

The captain looked at both of them with a questioning look on his face. Both Buck and Rachael started to speak at once and stopped, with Buck saying, "Ladies first."

Rachael started off, saying, "Not long ago I remember reading an article about the Coast Guard catching a submarine-like boat in the Gulf of Mexico. It was a two-man ship that floated submerged, with the exception of the view holes ticking out of the water. The low silhouette makes it hard to be picked up by visual, especially at night. They call them submersibles and they can carry up to 200 million dollars' worth of drugs inside. That's about three tons of drugs in one shipment being delivered all at once."

The captain thought about this, and then you could see the light come on in his head. At this point the sergeant called the captain over. "I think we found something here."

With that, Buck and Rachael followed the captain over to where the sergeant was standing. The sergeant pointed to the ground, and Collins was standing there, still with his headset on listening to the signal. The captain looked at the sergeant and asked, "What am I looking at, Sergeant?"

The sergeant kicked at a board partially covered with dirt and grass. The board moved and showed an opening below. The captain remembered reading about the tunnels used by the North Viet Cong during the Vietnam War and how they had whole bases of operations underground. He looked around and asked, "Somebody got a flashlight?"

Two of the soldiers came running up with flashlights in their hands and gave one to the captain as he asked, "Anybody want to go exploring in the dark?"

"How about we send Mateo, with him in the lead, just in case it's booby-trapped with bad stuff, Sir," said the sergeant.

"Good idea, and I'll go with you," Buck said.

Mateo was brought over in front of the opening in the ground and looked at the captain with a look of, what the hell are you going to do? The captain smiled and said, "You know what a tunnel rat is?"

Mateo shook his head no. The captain then said, "You're about to find out."

As the captain shined the light down into the darkness, he could make out a ladder on the side of the hole. Mateo looked at the captain. "Do I have a choice in this?"

The captain pulled his semi-auto out and pointed it at Mateo, who said at that point, "I didn't think so."

As Mateo made his way down the ladder, the captain followed down a minute later. When the captain hit bottom, he yelled up to Buck and said, "Come on down."

When Buck got to the bottom, all three of the men stood looking at what their flashlights could show them. The room they were standing in was about 20 feet wide and about 30 feet deep, with timbers holding the walls in place to keep them from caving in. The far end had a table and chairs with a computer laptop on it and a lantern above the table. Buck went over and struck a match and lit the lantern, which gave off more light than the flashlights could. Buck grabbed the lantern and used it to sweep the interior of the tunnel. On one side of the tunnel they found another opening that went back about another 20 feet. The opening was approximately six feet wide and expanded after you walked past the opening to about 10 feet wide. Buck shined the lantern into the opening and saw some stuff that kind of sparkled from the lantern light. Buck went into the opening, when the captain yelled, "Stop! Don't move an inch."

The captain walked over to where Buck was standing and said, "Look down."

Buck looked down and saw a string across the opening, realizing his foot was less than three inches from the string. Buck turned white as a sheet. The captain knelt down and, using his fingers, followed the string to an old claymore mine. Carefully cutting the string and disarming the claymore mine, the captain used his flashlight to look for more traps. Fortunately, it was the only one they found. Buck looked at the captain and said, "Thanks, Captain."

"Think nothing of it. We do the same thing for civilians, too."

With that, they both laughed and proceeded to see what was against the wall in this second room. The lights from the lantern and the flashlight shone on the opposite wall, and as they got closer, they were able to make out what they were looking at. At first, they couldn't believe it and then it struck them. This room was for the storage of drugs to be taken by submarine to the U.S. In front of them was a wall of drugs carefully wrapped in plastic and stacked against the wall. Mateo was looking at it as well, with a smile on his face, saying, "This looks like about two million dollars' worth of drugs down here."

The captain walked back to the mouth of the tunnel and handed the laptop to the sergeant. As he did so, he yelled up top to get some men to come down into the tunnel. With the sergeant barking orders, two men went down the ladder into the tunnel and assisted the captain and Buck in destroying the drugs along the back wall. They cut into the packages of drugs and dumped them on the ground. By the time they were done, they had destroyed 50 bricks of opium. They even had Mateo helping to destroy the packages of drugs, with tears in his eyes.

Then the captain ordered everyone out of the storage tunnel. Once everyone was clear, he threw a satchel charge down into the tunnel and ran for cover behind a group of rocks, covering his head, and waited. The explosion rocked the ground they were on, and the blast raised the dust and forest debris all around them. Once the dust and the debris settled, the captain got up and looked at where the tunnel used to be. In its place was a big hole 20 feet wide and 20 feet long in the ground.

The captain looked at Buck and Rachael and said, smiling, "You know they're going to be upset when they see the hole here and the drugs gone."

Buck and Rachael chuckled to themselves and got up, with everybody else looking at the hole in the ground where the storage area once was. The scouts came running into the opening to where the captain was standing. "The blast alerted the bad guys to us being here!"

"How many are there?"

"About 20, Sir, maybe more."

The captain looked at the sergeant and yelled, "Sergeant, you know what to do!"

With that, the sergeant started shouting orders, and the men set up a perimeter with their backs to the river. They used the jungle for cover and the uniforms made it easy for them to blend into the shadows. They created a flanking setup, where they would catch the bad guys in the middle in a cross fire situation. One of the soldiers climbed a tree and was their lookout to alert them when the bad guys showed up. Along with being the team's eyes, he also carried a sniper rifle.

In about five minutes the man in tree saw the cartel men coming down the trail. There were about 20 of them coming in a single file only because the trail was so narrow. As the cartel men made their way into the staging area, they bunched together in groups of four and five, while the others tried to come in from the jungle side. The team had themselves set up with two in each spot, one to watch the front and the other to protect the rear. The first group of the cartel came running into the center of the area and never knew what hit them. Two of the cartel men fell without being able to see who had killed them. The others that survived the first five seconds of the battle fired blindly into the jungle.

Those who tried to circle around through the jungle were caught by the rear guard in each position, falling in place as they were hit by the bullets. The ones that escaped running down the trail were taken out by the sniper in the tree. One of the cartel men who was running down the trail escaped into the jungle and was able to get away. The sniper reported to the sergeant about the one getting away. The captain asked the sergeant for a count of the team. After about five minutes of checking by the sergeant, he was happy to report that all of the team were still in one piece. Rachael and Buck were with the captain at the time of the firefight and were still in one piece as well. The bad news was that Mateo took a round in the shoulder. The sergeant and the team medic were working on him. The captain walked over to Mateo to check on him, and finding the bullet went through the muscle and had missed the bone completely, he was somewhat relieved. The captain told the men to take the bodies and put them into the hole where the tunnel used to be. The team stacked the 19 bodies on top of each other. That way it would be a reminder to the cartel to not use it as a staging area or build there again.

With the body drop done the captain said, "I'm pleased with your actions in the firefight, especially not getting shot."

The men laughed at the comment about being shot. The sergeant joined in the praise. "I know it's been a long trip this time, but I'm proud of each and every one of you."

A moment later one of the soldiers on guard called out to the team, saying there was a man with a white handkerchief coming down the trail, waving it as he walked. The other soldiers took a defensive position and waited to see what would happen next. The captain, with Buck and Rachael, waited in the clearing to see who this guy was. When the man walked into the area where the captain was standing, he called out, "Don't shoot; I'm on your side."

The captain waited a moment until the man flashed his badge, showing he was a DEA agent. The captain, still not sure, held his rifle on the guy as he continued to talk.

Buck said to the captain, "Ask him his name."

Hearing Buck tell this to the captain, the man said, "My name is Jose Jimenez and I want to be an astronaut."

With that Buck said, "He's for real; the name he gave you was the one we were told to look for before we left Miami."

The agent looked relieved that he was believed, and he stood there for a moment collecting his thoughts.

"Have you been following us?" the captain asked.

"Yes, I've been following you for the last couple of days," the agent replied.

By now the rest of the team came out of the jungle, walking up to the captain.

The agent looked around. "No wonder the cartel men didn't make it back alive. Oh, by the way, there is another group coming down the river. They'll be here in about 10 minutes, tops."

The captain looked at the agent, "When were you going to tell us about the men coming down the river?"

"As soon as I knew you weren't going to shoot me."

"I guess I don't blame you for that," The captain laughed.

"Captain, if you can try and save the boat, we could use it to get back to civilization," said the agent.

"Good idea. Alright, you heard the request. Try not to blow up the boat; it means the difference of riding or walking back through the jungle."

The sergeant took control over the team and had them take spots along the riverfront in the shadows behind the trees. When the sergeant felt sure his men were ready, he reported back to the captain, "The men are ready, Sir."

With Buck and Rachael in position everybody waited for the boat to show. In about five minutes you could hear the motor of the boat as it made its way down the river. The eyes of the team in one of the trees whistled down to the sergeant to let him know they were on their way. The sergeant yelled out to the team, "Make your shots count!"

By now Buck and Rachael were counting the bullets that they had left for their own weapons; each of them had one full clip left. The size of the landing party would determine if they had enough for the firefight. The sniper in the tree whistled again and with his fingers gave a count of how many were aboard the boat. Showing both hands once meant that there were 10 cartel men aboard the boat. As the team waited, all you could hear were the sounds of the jungle with the boat motor in the background. The boat motor stopped and the cartel men started rowing the boat so as not to give away their position on the river. The boat slid in quietly next to the shack by the river. Each cartel man was given directions by the lead man in front of the boat as to where he wanted them to be. As each man got on shore via the dock, the team slowly turned around to face them. The leader of the cartel saw the bodies of the first group and swore that he would kill every one of the men who had done this. The sniper waited until he finished his statement, and putting the crosshairs of his scope on the head of the leader, he fired. At first the cartel was surprised to see the leader's head disappear in a mist of red as he fell to the ground. The cartel men looked everywhere, firing as they attempted to find cover. As each of the cartel men made for cover in the jungle, they were cut down in their tracks. The sniper kept firing at the ones running for the boat. His aim was deadly and effective. Some of the cartel men who were able to find cover started firing at anything that moved. Most of the survivors were hiding behind the bodies that were stacked in the hole. Buck and Rachael, with the captain, placed their shots carefully at the men, who were using the bodies for cover. After a minute, the second firefight was over. The sergeant did a check on his men and reported back to the captain, all's good for the team. The team took the 10 bodies of the cartel men and loaded them on top of the other cartel men and left them to rot in the sun. When everything was back to normal, the captain had the sergeant load the team onto the boat and shoved off the shore and started down the river, heading north. Buck and Rachael told the captain that this would be their last trip with the team and that they would be heading back to Miami from the "vacation" they had been on.

"No problem, glad to have you around for the fun," the captain said.

They reached the helicopter in about three hours' time. In fact, the flight crew had barely got comfortably seated before the team showed up. The helicopter lifted off an hour later, making its way to the Panama City airport. When they landed at the airport, a Military C-130 was parked and waiting for the team, with Buck and Rachael ready to fly home to America. The pilot and the copilot were ready and waiting for the team to show up, compliments of the wizzo calling ahead to let them know they were on their way back to Panama.

The DEA agent stayed in a hotel in Panama for a couple of days before he called his handler to let him know that he was okay, just so he could enjoy the finer things in life--for a little while, anyway.

The team with Buck and Rachael left from the helicopter directly to the C-130, and as the engines started up, they settled into the cargo seats for the ride home to Miami. Upon landing at the air base south of Miami, they all got off and loaded into the blue school bus waiting for them, with another truck for the gear following them off the flight line to their own quarters.

Buck and Rachael were met by Evans and Linda, with Miguel pacing back and forth in excitement. Miguel ran out to them when he saw them leave the plane. He didn't know whether to hug both of them or shake hands with them, and as they stood talking on the flight line, Evans and Linda walked out to meet them. Upon seeing them, Buck and Rachael both stood there and smiled. "It was a hell of a vacation, and to make matters worse, we ran out of suntan lotion," Buck said.

Evans and Linda laughed and hugged each one of them. Miguel was still not sure what to do but was carrying what luggage they had brought back with them, which at this point was next to nothing. It was like old home week for all of them.

"The debriefing will be tomorrow, but tonight it's dinner on us," Evans said.

"If anything on the menu even has the words MRE on it, there will be a homicide in the restaurant," Buck replied.

Rachael seconded the motion by saying, "I'll make sure whoever it is, is down for good."

They all laughed as they made their way to the car. Evans and Linda dropped them off at the same hotel they had been in previously and, in fact, the same room as before.

"Enjoy yourselves until dinner time. We'll pick you up at 7:00 pm. Miguel will stay with us until dinner time," Evans told Buck.

As they drove away, Buck and Rachael watched the car get into the traffic of the city. They went into the hotel foyer and asked the front desk for a key to their room. They made their way to the second floor and opened the door to their room. Walking in, they saw a fruit basket on the counter and chocolate candies on the pillows of their bed. Rachael opened the closets and noticed a new dress and a suit for each of them, with shoes to wear for tonight.

Rachael looked at Buck. "It seems they thought of everything for us."

Buck looked inside the closet. "Wow, they really did think of everything, didn't they?"

Both of them took a shower and let the water run down their backs as they stood there letting the aches and pains of the trip wash away. Feeling refreshed, they opened the chest of drawers below the TV and found clean underwear and a note saying, "We're glad you're home."

Rachael showed the note to Buck. They both sat together on the bed and cried. The tears were tears of relief and the shock of being in the real world again. As they lay there, they fell asleep together, knowing for the first time they didn't have to worry about being killed or sleeping with one eye open all the time.

When seven o'clock came, they were dressed in the new clothes that were in the hotel room, and both of them came down the elevator refreshed and ready to eat. Miguel met them in the foyer and took them to the car, where Evans and Linda were waiting. They went to a fancy restaurant and had a good dinner, and they all enjoyed themselves. Buck and Rachael were amazed that there was real silverware to use and clean glasses to drink from. When dinner was over, Evans and Linda drove them back to their hotel and dropped them off, once more saying, "We'll have someone pick you up at eight o'clock tomorrow morning." With that, everybody said goodnight and went their separate ways.

The next morning Buck and Rachael were downstairs, waiting in the foyer, when the car came to pick them up to take them to the federal building. After arriving at the federal building, they went through the metal detectors where Evans and Linda were waiting for them on the other side. They were escorted to Evans' office, where they sat with a secretary taking notes and a video camera filming the debriefing. After the debriefing was done, Evans and Linda told them the good news about what they had accomplished in the work they did in Colombia and Honduras. The Colombian government was happy with the destruction of the poppy fields, the finding of the double agent in Bogota', and the apprehension of Mateo, who with a little help told them about the drug operations in Southeast Asia and was willing to testify against the kingpin for leniency.

And with that, their time in Miami came to a close. The next day Buck and Rachael, with Miguel, flew back to Phoenix and to their own home in Smith County, overlooking the Chiricahua Mountains.

It had been three weeks from the start of this "vacation" to the time they came home. When they went to work the following day, the deputies and staff were happy to see them. They told everybody it was nice to be back so they could rest from their "vacation." Everybody laughed when they said that, but inside Buck and Rachael knew they meant every word.

The End

EPILOGUE

The captain and his team were given a Presidential Citation award for their work in apprehending the Kingpin and the Bookkeeper. The team also received other medals for their work in destroying the poppy fields, destroying over 10 million dollars of opium before it arrived into the United States, and finding a double agent who was terminated before any other agents could be hurt or worse.

The captain was promoted to major for the above actions and took over as the commander of training for the counter drug operations school at the Special Forces training base at Fort Bragg, North Carolina. The sergeant was assigned there as a specialist instructor still working for the Major.

The warehouse in Mexico was burnt to the ground with 300 million dollars of heroin, cocaine and marijuana burned in the fire. No one knows how the fire started to this day.

The Monterrey Cartel is still operating, but with a far less impact on the streets in the US. Having no real leadership due to the in-fighting and other cartels trying to take over their territory, they were eventually swallowed up by other groups trying to cash in on their demise. The drugs flowing into the United States was impacted so much the street price doubled for a period of six months before bottoming out again.

The kingpin was found guilty for just about everything the federal government could throw at him, to include murder, money laundering, the RICO act, selling of drugs etc...., He will be spending the rest of his life in a maximum-security prison in Colorado with no chance of parole.

The kingpin's family was sent back to Mexico to live out their lives in the house the kingpin built, knowing that they will never see their husband and father ever again. They too are now living in fear that they may become one of the statistics of the dead people in the drug war that continues throughout Mexico.

George Rasmussen was found guilty for treason and selling secrets against the United States to the cartel. His argument for doing so was because he was being blackmailed for using drugs while he was stationed at the U.S. embassy in Columbia. He is in prison at the same maximum security prison in Colorado as the kingpin. (Who knows they may be bunkies in the same cell.)

The bookkeeper was sentenced to federal prison for RICO violations and money laundering. He is serving his time at a federal detention center in Florida.

Mateo Diaz was found guilty of drug distribution and RICO violations. He received a more lenient sentence for testifying against the kingpin and is still being called on by the Federal prosecutors for his knowledge of the drug business in South East Asia. He is serving his time at the federal detention facility in Florida. (Who knows maybe the bookkeeper and Mateo are bunkies as well.)

The secretary was transferred to a less classified position to continue as a secretary in another office. Her grandparents still live in Bogota' with family, friends and relatives.

Miguel was awarded his American citizenship within three months of his arrival into the United States. The reason for such a short time was for saving Buck and Rachael's life twice. (The FBI assisted in getting the INS services to speed it through without the typical red tape.) Miguel, having received his GED, is currently enrolled at Arizona State University where he is working on a degree in law enforcement with a minor in Political Science.

Evans and Linda were married in October as they had planned. Buck, Rachael and Miguel were there to be the best man and maid of honor and to help celebrate their marriage. Miguel was the ring bearer for the wedding. They were both transferred and promoted to Washington DC and now work in the FBI building when not tending their twins.

Buck and Rachael were given a special letter of appreciation from the FBI for their work in Honduras and Columbia and a letter from the President of United States personally thanking them for their contribution in the fight against the drug cartels.